The

Ninety
Fifth

Book design by:
Arbor Services, Inc.
www.arborservices.co/

Printed in the United States of America

The Ninety Fifth
Emily Sam

1. Title 2. Author 3. Fiction

Library of Congress Control Number: 2017918131
ISBN 13: 978-0-692-98147-4

The Ninety Fifth

EMILY SAM

KalKat Publishing

*I would like to thank my mom
for all her encouragement and support.*

Contents

Chapter One

Fort DeRussy Beach was beautiful, rain or shine. The rugged slopes of O'ahu framed the beach, where the land gave way to brilliant blue water and the jagged outline of the reef below. Palm trees and banyans stood along the road leading from the fort to the shore. Even on the hottest days a cool breeze blew in from the sea.

I dug my toes into the white sand beach and tried to lose myself in the salt breeze and the sunlight. The thing that fascinated me most about the ocean was the way it was always changing. Sometimes we saw dolphins in the waves, or caught glimpses of giant sea turtles floating just offshore, or found little fragments of driftwood and sea glass washed up along the high tide line beside the usual scraps of old seaweed and battered wood. A calm surf could whip into waves in a matter of moments. I loved that mutability.

I'd been unpredictable like that, once, but then I'd grown up.

"Look at me, Mommy!" shrieked my three-year-old daughter Lydia, splashing in the waves. Her older brother, Conrad, was building a sandcastle. He'd used too much water in the mixture, and every time he moved on to the next turret, the last one slid sideways and collapsed into the moat.

"I'm watching," I called back. I sat in the shade of our beach umbrella with the baby, Margie, who was napping on the beach towel beside me.

My children had grown up on Hawaii. They took the saltwater and the endless summer for granted. I'd been raised on the East Coast. I knew how lucky I was.

Margie gurgled in her sleep and then began to cry. I lifted her into my lap, which was almost lost under my growing belly, to rub her back. After a moment, she quieted.

I'd have loved Hawaii as a teenager. I'd have dared my friends to sneak onto the beach at night and skinny-dip, drink beer filched from my mother's fridge, and kiss two boys I liked on the same night without making any promises to either of them.

It wasn't so long ago that I'd been eighteen, but I had changed a lot since then. I wanted so badly to become the kind of woman who could make my husband, Marcus, proud.

Another breeze blew in, this one cooler. Grey, low-hanging clouds crept in along the horizon.

"Conrad! Lydia! Come here!" I called, scooping my youngest into the two-seat stroller. The older children ran back, shrieking, the plastic pail and matching shovel dangling from Conrad's hand. Lydia crawled into the second seat, which left me with one hand to push the stroller, one hand to balance the umbrella on top, and Conrad to trot along after me on foot. My hands were always full nowadays. I was still getting used to that.

When I looked back over my shoulder, I could see a wall of rain advancing across the sea toward us.

"Race you home," I told Conrad, and we took off toward our house in the kind of slow-motion speed walk that passes for running when it comes to pregnant women and small boys. Lydia laughed. I could hear the rain pounding across the surface of the Pacific as it drew closer. We reached the house at the same time as the storm.

• • • •

I was due in two months, and I was already enormous. Ultrasounds had confirmed my suspicion that I was carrying twins. Margie had only turned one a few months ago, which meant that I would be juggling three babies before the end of the summer.

Marcus was due to be deployed to Iraq in three months. He'd be gone for over a year.

This was the life I'd chosen, and the man I'd chosen to share it with. *This We'll Defend.*

I traded my bathing suit for a loose dress, then wrestled the kids into some clean clothes. I'd have killed for an old T-shirt and sweatpants, but I couldn't go out dressed like that. Makeup, too, was a must.

Is anybody actually impressed by this? I wondered as I wrestled a pair of black flats onto my swollen feet.

In the military community, it is the solemn duty of a colonel's wife to appear in control at all times. Just as Marcus was a leader among the men, I held a position of rank among the army wives. When I went grocery shopping, I wasn't simply buying food for my family. I was representing my husband and the army in which he served.

I gathered up our grocery bags and then herded my children, dressed in clean clothes and refreshed from a rainy-day nap, toward the door. Three pairs of shoes were coerced onto three small feet, and departure was imminent, when we heard a knock at the door.

"One minute," I called.

"I'll get it!" announced Conrad, and he yanked the door open wide.

The woman standing on the other side was tall and blonde, dressed in a fitted floral-print cotton dress.

"Naomi," I said, surprised. We were neighbors and had become friendly with each other, but I hadn't been expecting a visitor.

She took in the kids, the bags, and the shopping list in one glance. She was a mother too, and understood that any outing with a carload of kids was a logistical production.

"Sorry," she said. "I'm interrupting. The boys are at a birthday party until four. I thought . . . but never mind."

"No!" I said, before she could turn away. "There's no rush. Anyway, it looks like it might rain again. You shouldn't walk home in that."

Naomi looked up. The sky was blue, and she smiled at my obvious fumble. "I just want a few minutes. Without Marcus here. I needed to talk to someone who'd understand."

"Come in," I insisted, steering Conrad and Lydia back into the house. "We'll watch an episode of Thomas."

"Thomas!" crowed Lydia. "Hooray!"

I arranged the kids in front of the TV, with Margie in her bouncy chair and the other two sprawled on the carpet. Naomi hovered in the kitchen until I returned.

"Oof," I said, "sorry, I'm moving slower these days. Can I get you something?"

Naomi sat down. "That isn't necessary. I'll only be a few minutes."

"No, please, let me get you some water, or . . ."

"Rob's leaving me," said Naomi.

I turned to her. She stared down at her hands, unwilling to make eye contact with me. Someone who didn't know her better might have thought she looked calm, but I could see the quiver in her lower lip and the pinched tightness at the corners of her eyes.

"What happened?" I asked, sitting down beside her and putting my hand on hers. Naomi was as good as I was at playing the game. Every colonel's wife has to know how. But she wasn't a colonel's wife anymore, was she?

I'd complained to myself about having to follow the rules, but in that moment I knew that I'd happily play the game until the day I died, as long as it meant that I got to keep Marcus.

"I'm not sure. Everything was fine. I thought it was fine." Naomi let out a shuddering sigh, but she kept her voice steady. "When Rob deployed, he seemed distant. When he left, he told me he'd count the days until he came back, but he stopped answering my messages a couple of weeks ago and I just assumed he was busy . . . until I got the papers."

"No explanation?" I asked.

"Nothing."

"Oh, Naomi, I'm sorry . . ."

"Don't," she said, pulling her hand away. "I know you mean well, but I don't need pity. I just—I had to tell someone."

"I'm glad you did," I murmured. "If there's anything I can do . . ." I trailed off, not sure what else to say. What could I possibly do for her? I couldn't change Rob's mind. I couldn't fix their marriage.

Naomi was thinking along the same lines. She looked so fragile in that pale dress with its oversized rose pattern, like a china doll that somebody had dropped and all her joints had broken. For a few seconds I both hoped and feared that she would break down right there and I'd have to comfort her. I wanted to make her feel better, but a horrible voice inside me kept chanting, *Better you than me, better you than me*, and as awful as that was, I couldn't deny that I felt that way.

She didn't break. She raised herself straighter, then got to her feet. "I have to go," she said. "The kids will be home soon."

"Do they know?" I asked.

She shook her head. "I don't know how to explain it. I'll tell them eventually. No hurry, I guess." Her smile was bitter.

"Really, if there's anything I can do, call me."

Naomi looked at her reflection in the microwave door and wiped a smear of eyeliner away. "I will," she said, but I was sure she wouldn't. "Keep it to yourself for a while, okay? I want to keep things normal for as long as I can. At least until the kids know."

I nodded, and Naomi picked up her purse from where it lay in a heap on the table. I got up, shuffling awkwardly after her as she retreated toward the front hall.

"Good luck," I said as she left.

"Too late for that, isn't it?" she asked with a sickly smile, and then she was gone.

• • • •

When Marcus came home that night, I had the kids working on a craft project in the living room while I finished dinner.

I was cutting up tomatoes for the salad, but my mind wasn't on the work. I kept picturing Naomi's face and how she managed to hide almost everything. When I was younger, I would have encouraged her to cry or scream or smash something, whatever would help. Now I wanted everything to be clean and tidy. If I couldn't have that, I wanted things to at least *seem* clean and tidy.

Marcus touched my shoulder and I jumped, nearly slicing the tips of my fingers off.

"Sorry!" he said. "I didn't mean to startle you."

I stood on my toes to meet his kiss. "Just thinking."

"Thinking hard." He leaned against the counter and looked down, examining my face carefully. I liked that Marcus was so observant and intent most of the time, but not tonight. I didn't want him to know what was on my mind.

"I was thinking that the car won't work with five kids." I rubbed my belly to indicate the twins. "We'll need a minivan before long. We should sort that out before you leave."

"You're worried," said Marcus. "About the tour."

Among other things. "Fifteen months in Iraq? Of course I'm worried." I kissed him again. "But I'll figure it out, and I know you'll be okay."

"We've gotten through this before." He laid his hand on my stomach and smiled. "You've got this covered, Amy. I know you do."

He was a natural father, my husband. I just sometimes wished he weren't so . . . dad-ish. I wished I could tell him how lost I'd felt lately, but what could he possibly do? Maybe it would plant the idea in his head that I was unhappy, that we were unhappy. Maybe the idea would gnaw at the back of his mind for months until, somewhere in the deserts of the Middle East, he would decide that he wanted a different life and a better wife, and serve me divorce papers from half a world away, like Rob had done to Naomi.

"You're right," I said, turning back to the cutting board. "I was just being silly."

"Feeling vulnerable isn't silly," said Marcus, rubbing my back.

Maybe it wasn't silly, but *vulnerable* is not in the vocabulary of a military wife.

• • • •

The girls arrived.

Marcus left.

I drove the new minivan loaded with our five kids to the store, to school, to the beach. For fifteen months I wondered, *Will he come home to me?* A bullet could take him. Or a landmine. Or just the distance between us, wider than the mere miles that separated his base and mine.

Chapter Two

Marcus left in the fall and came back the next winter.

Although I'd grown used to the temperate climate of Waikiki, I missed the icy desperate thrill of Northern winters, the wished-for relief of snow days, and thawing inside with hot chocolate after rushing through streets so cold your eyelashes froze.

That's pretty sick, Amy, I thought, stepping out into winter weather so mild it hardly required long sleeves. The kids were practically crawling over themselves they were so eager to see Marcus.

The twins kept looking at each other. "Daddy?" they asked each other. "Daddy?" Their father was a mystery to them, someone they only knew from Skype calls and family lore. As far as they were concerned, he was a man in a photograph, two-dimensional and permanently absent.

Conrad, almost seven, was the most excited. He'd been trapped in a house with too many girls for too long.

"Is that him?" he asked, every time a car drove by.

"Not yet," I said. "You'll know when it's him."

At last the car pulled up. Marcus got out, still talking with the driver, and grinned when he saw us. A dignified wife, wanting to impress anyone who might happen to see, would have walked up to him and given him a gracious lingering hug. I ran to him and crushed him to me as hard as I could.

The driver smiled at us, saluted, and pulled away.

"Are you crying?" asked Marcus. "Amy, it's okay. I'm here."

The children, so recently excited, had gone quiet the moment their father arrived. When Marcus turned to them, Conrad dashed up and gave him a silent hug. Lydia followed a little less enthusiastically.

"Aren't you going to say hello to your father?" I asked.

Margie approached, then ran to me and hid behind my knees.

"That's okay," said Marcus. "It's been a long time, hasn't it, Margie? I won't bite, kiddo. Come here."

As Marcus knelt down, she crept out, kissed him briefly on the cheek, then ran back to me.

Marcus turned to the twins. "Eliza, Alice. How are you?" He said it warmly, looking at each girl in turn. I'd sent a lot of pictures, and Marcus had figured out how to tell them apart, even though he hadn't seen them in person since they were infants.

As we headed back inside, Marcus put his arm around me. I'd missed being touched by an adult—it had been over a year. Aside from cursory contact, such as handshakes and the accidental brush of fingers when money changed hands, I'd only been touched by the kids. It was a relief to be held by someone simply because they loved me, not because they needed something from me. I wanted to melt into Marcus and let that feeling linger.

Sitting down to dinner was like eating with a guest. I'd made steak and spinach, potatoes and corn, the kind of celebratory dinner I'd have fixed before we came to the island. I was pushing the limits of what the local grocery store offered. I was usually stuck with whatever had come in the most recent shipment and hadn't been snapped up by the locals who knew exactly when the shelves were stocked and didn't have to herd five children wherever they went. Grocery shopping in the middle of the Pacific wasn't like shopping on the mainland.

I served myself a half portion. I'd tried to lose a little weight before Marcus got back, but I hadn't had time to dedicate myself to any serious weight loss.

"How's school?" Marcus asked.

"Okay," said Conrad.

"Just okay? Don't you have any friends? Do anything fun? Learn anything?"

Conrad poked at his spinach. "Zach."

"What's Zach like?"

"He's okay."

Marcus gave up and turned to Lydia. "What about you? Your mom told me you like art class. What's your favorite project so far?"

Lydia looked up at him with wide eyes. "I drew a tiger."

"A tiger? Do you like tigers?"

Lydia's eyes slid to her brother. "They're okay."

Before long, I found myself talking just to fill the silence. I told Marcus things I'd already told him in emails and phone calls over the last few months. Marcus spoke a little, but he'd been in a war zone, and besides not having much to say in front of the kids, I knew it always took him a little while to adjust to being home.

After dessert—fresh starfruit and tangerines, two of the perks of Hawaiian winter—I herded the kids upstairs to begin the lengthy process of getting ready for bed. Marcus put a hand on my shoulder before I could follow.

"I've got this," he said. "They need a chance to get used to me again, and you could use a break. Let me take care of it."

I hesitated. While Marcus was gone, we'd developed a routine. We all knew the routine, what battles could and could not be won, the order in which everyone got to use the bathroom . . .

"Sure," I said. "Thank you."

Marcus went upstairs, kissing me as he passed, and I started cleaning the kitchen.

Sometimes I felt like I was never satisfied. When I was alone, I wanted someone to help me. When I had help, I wanted to be in charge.

Maybe what I really wanted was the freedom to ask for help or refuse it—the freedom to choose, rather than to be told. I washed the dishes, wiped down the counters, and tried to stay busy until I couldn't stand it any longer and finally made my way upstairs.

Marcus sat on Alice and Eliza's bed, the girls in his lap, the other kids squashed into the bed beside him. He was reading, doing voices for each character, and the kids were howling with laughter, even though I'd probably read them the same book fifty times and they knew every word by heart.

When he was finished, Marcus looked up to see me watching. I looked around the room, trying to guess what parts of the nighttime ritual had been missed.

"Hungry!" crowed Eliza, shoving her favorite book, *The Very Hungry Caterpillar*, into Marcus's hands. My husband looked at me, and after a moment I realized that he was waiting for permission.

"Go for it," I said. "As long as you're willing to read, they'll ask for another story."

Marcus opened the book, and I stepped out of the room, closing the door behind me as my husband gave a dramatic performance of a story I knew by rote. I could sympathize with that caterpillar, who was never satisfied.

You're selfish, I told myself. *Don't you want what's best for your family? You're worried about brushed teeth and clean pajamas and getting them up in time for breakfast, and all they want is to be happy.*

● ● ● ●

I was ready for bed by the time Marcus came in. I lay staring at the ceiling while I waited, trying to make sense of my thoughts.

"Hey there," he said, wiggling his eyebrows at me, and he kissed me deep and slow. "Did you miss me?"

"Every day," I answered.

"How much?" he asked, tracing the curve of my ear with his fingers and nuzzling my throat.

I reached for the top button of his shirt. "I didn't think you were in any hurry. How many times did you read *The Very Hungry Caterpillar?*"

"Twice. Eliza wanted to hear it again, but I told her that mommy needed me." He tugged at his shirt, impatient with my progress on the buttons. "Urgently."

"You were right," I said, slid my arms around his neck, and pulled him down to me.

As a girl, I'd enjoyed my freedom. Why would anyone get married? It sounded dull. How could you want to spend every day with the same person for the rest of your life? With Marcus, I understood. Marriage hadn't reduced our passion for each other. We'd each taken the time to learn what the other liked, and his lengthy absences during deployments only honed that passion. My desire for him was more than physical. When he ran his hands down the length of my body, reaching for the hem of my nightdress and tracing his fingers up the curve of my thigh, I didn't just want a man. I wanted Marcus, his familiar smell and the sound of his ragged breathing in my ear. The thing we'd built between us was strong and steady. As a teenager, I'd wanted to explore. As a woman, I longed to visit my favorite familiar places with the man I loved.

Afterward, when we lay wrapped up in each other, I slowed my breathing and closed my eyes.

"I missed you so much," said Marcus, lifting himself up on one elbow so that he could kiss me again. "Is it hard? When I'm not here?"

"You mean, do I get lonely?" I asked, stroking his arm.

"That, too," he said, grinning. He ran his fingers through my hair and sighed. "I love my job, Amy. But my whole life is here, with you, and I can't be part of it when I'm away. At least I have the comfort of knowing that you'll hold everything together while I'm off . . ." He paused. "Doing what I do."

"I know it's hard on you, too," I said. "I know you've seen things—"

"I don't want to talk about that. Not because I want to keep it from you. I just don't want any of, you know, any of *that* to come home with me. I want this to be a safe place. I want you to be safe."

"I'm safe with you," I said.

Marcus smiled, kissed my forehead, and rolled out of bed. He went into the bathroom and came out brushing his teeth.

"I've missed this," he said through the toothpaste. "Normal stuff. Dinner, and bedtime, and you . . ." He winked. "I've missed everything."

"I've tried my best to hold down the fort," I said. "Keeping the home fires burning and all that. It's not the same without you, though. We're missing our most important piece when you're gone."

"Oh, uh huh . . ." Marcus held a finger up to tell me, *one moment.* He disappeared into the bathroom and came back a moment later with empty hands and nothing on. He was in even better shape than he'd been when he left, with his caramel skin taught across his stomach, his broad shoulders, toned arms, and fit legs . . . I pulled the blanket up to hide the shape of my own body and moved over to make room for him beside me.

Instead he sat down on the end of the bed. "I was waiting to discuss this in person. We'll most likely be relocated soon. I need to get some more information, but it's in the works."

"Oh." I mulled this over. "Where are we going?"

"Back East. Why?" He grinned. "Were you hoping for Europe?"

"Europe could be beautiful," I hedged. "What did they tell you?"

"They're sending me to do some specialized training," Marcus said. "I think that something big is coming up, and they want me on the team. I don't know too much yet, but it sounds like a great opportunity." He grimaced. "I'd tell you more, but you know how it is."

"I get it," I said. "You can't talk about it."

"I wish I could," he said, rubbing my bare leg. "I hate having secrets from you."

"It will be strange to be back East," I said.

"Are you happy?"

"I like it here," I told him, "but I've missed some people." I was still trying to figure out how I really felt. Pleased? Indifferent? It was too early to say.

"Good." He looked relieved. "I know that it will be an adjustment for the kids and that a lot of that falls on you. But you'll feel more at home, I think. We'll be closer to our families, too. It will be good for all of us."

I looked at him, and as much as I loved him, I realized that what I felt was exhaustion. It wasn't that I particularly loved living in Hawaii, and I'd known when I married Marcus that we'd move wherever and whenever the needs of the army warranted. Anyway, what did I have to lose? Aside from Naomi, I hadn't made many connections at Fort DeRussy. My family had been my whole life. As long as Marcus and the kids were with me, nothing would change.

Which was kind of the problem. I needed a change. We'd moved to Hawaii for Marcus's career, and now we were moving back East for Marcus's schooling. What about what I needed?

"All right," I said at last. "I'll start packing."

"A woman of action," said Marcus, patting my legs. "That's my wife."

I reached for him, but already that perfectly happy feeling of having Marcus back was fading. When I kissed him, I knew that my husband wasn't the problem. I was the problem.

If anyone had to change to make me happier, it was me.

• • • •

Corrina drove from New York City for a visit shortly after the army moved us to our new house.

Corrina wasn't the kind of mother you could call *Mom*. People who met us often didn't guess that we were related, partly because of our appearance, but mostly because of our demeanors.

True to form, she arrived three hours later than she'd said she was coming, at the same time as the new furniture. She drifted in without knocking, examining the arrangement of our furniture with raised eyebrows.

"Am I in the right place?" she asked.

No, Corrina, I wanted to say, *we're all just hanging out in a stranger's house and telling the movers where to put their furniture. Our place is three doors down.*

"You sure are," said Marcus, adopting the warm, fatherly tone he always used around my mother. I wasn't sure if he wanted to impress her or if the shift in his mannerisms was unconscious.

"Lovely house," said Corrina without bothering to look around. "Now, who do we have here? Conrad, you've gotten so big. And is this little Lydia? Not so little anymore. Come give Nonna Corrina a hug."

The children stared at her with saucer eyes. To them, she must have looked like something out of a fairy tale. A witch, maybe, or an elfin apparition. Rings glistened on every finger, and her brightly beaded necklace hung to the middle of her floor-length kurta. Her naturally curly red hair, now streaked with grey highlights, fell halfway down her back. To children raised in an orderly military household, this close encounter with their free-spirited grandmother must have been borderline surreal.

When they didn't approach, Corrina went to them, hugging each of them for a long moment. She stepped back when she got to Margie, raising her hands to either side of her own face in theatrical surprise. "Why, dear, your aura is lovely!" She put her hands on Margie's cheeks. "And don't you look just like your mother did at your age?" Margie shrugged helplessly and allowed herself to be hugged.

"Now, before we get started, would you give me a tour?" She put her arm through mine and winked at me. "And perhaps we'll have time for a private word."

I managed not to roll my eyes and led her to our bedroom. The movers had set up our bed, but I'd had to replace a lot of our clothes and blankets after the move. We'd brought the kids' favorite clothes, their favorite books, our photos, and a dozen beloved toys. As for my own clothes, I planned to lose forty pounds by the time summer rolled around and it was warm enough to unpack the dresses and light blouses that I could wear year-round in Waikiki. Most of my new purchases hadn't been put away yet and stood around the edges of the wall or lay draped across the night tables.

Corrina sat down on the edge of the bed. Her feet didn't reach the floor, and she swung them back and forth in an almost childlike manner as she looked around. In a lot of ways, I thought of her as a child. Growing up, my sister and I had taken as much care of her as she had of us. She was a free spirit, my mother. She was the model of motherhood I'd rejected with my own family.

"Lots of light in this house," she said. "Plenty of windows. Wonderful energy flow. You'll be happy here, I'm sure of it."

"Great," I said. "I'll keep that in mind."

"Now, is something troubling you? You seem somewhat off."

"I'm great. Maybe a bit tired, but that's normal these days."

"Do you ever get any *me* time? All these kids, and yes dear, you have a lovely family, but it all seems like a lot of work." This line of questioning was typical of my mother. Corrina lived to please herself. Duty, obligation, and responsibility were three arguments that didn't often sway her. "Do you ever do anything just for yourself?"

I tried to adopt Marcus's patient tone. "I'm living the life I chose. This *is* what I want to do."

"Then why don't you seem happy?"

I flinched. Corrina might live a dreamy life, but she wasn't totally oblivious. There wasn't much I could tell her about my choices that would make sense to her. She was honest in her opinions to a fault, not a sensitive motherly type.

"Things are hard when Marcus is away. And I have been feeling fat lately," I blurted.

Corrina looked me up and down. "Fat? I don't think so, dear. Plump, maybe. Curvy. Yes, curvy."

"Thanks," I said drily.

"Oh, men love a curvy woman," insisted Corrina.

My mother was twice-divorced, but I didn't ask the source of this advice on what men liked in a woman. "I've been looking into getting a band fitted," I said instead.

"Band?" My mother knit her eyebrows. "You're talking about a surgery?"

"I'm talking about forty or fifty pounds," I said. "I don't see what my options are."

"Exercise. Go running. Take up yoga." Corrina waved a jeweled hand dismissively. "You don't need some surgeon poking around. *Reader's Digest* had a story the other month . . ."

"I don't have time to work out," I said. I pulled my shirt tight to accentuate the shape of my belly. "I don't have an hour a day to spend at the gym, and I don't have the energy to go for a run before the kids get up. I'm a full-time mother. My kids are my life."

I hoped that Corrina might get the hint, that I was trying to be the mother that I'd wished for when I was little. Instead, she gave me a sad look.

We heard a knock at the door, and Marcus poked his head in. "Sorry to interrupt. They're bringing in the things for the living room and want to know where to put the couch."

"Marcus, come in," said my mother. "Amy just told me that she's thinking about having surgery."

Marcus looked at me and stepped into the room. "Is something wrong?" he asked in a low voice, in case the kids were listening.

I folded my arms over my stomach. "I just said that I'm thinking about getting a lap band."

"Why?" asked Marcus, genuinely baffled.

"Oh, good," said Corrina. "I thought maybe you'd said something to her, that she needed to change how she looks."

"Of course not. You're a good-looking woman," said Marcus. "What do you want to have surgery for?"

Good-looking? In college, I'd been hot. Did he somehow miss that his praise was only lukewarm?

"I need to drop forty pounds," I said. "I haven't had time to focus on myself, with the kids and the house and keeping everything running . . ." I trailed off. This was a mantra I'd repeated to myself for weeks, months even, but I hated having to say it aloud.

Marcus considered this. His eyes bounced from me, to my mother, then back to me. "We can talk about it later?"

Corrina sniffed. "It doesn't seem right to me, but if that's what you really want, it's your choice, dear." She hopped off the bed and smoothed the sheets down to erase the wrinkles she'd made there.

"Thank you," I said, trying and failing to hide my sarcasm.

"Oh, don't do that." She waved again, brushing my words away. "You're the one who has to live with whatever you choose to do."

I waited until she left the room before taking a deep breath. She hadn't been an awful mother, just an inconsistent one. Still, it bothered me that the voice in my head so often sounded like her. *Do something for yourself.* Well, that's exactly what I was doing.

"Where did this come from?" asked Marcus, hanging back with me. "Is something wrong?"

I took his hand. "The better I look, the better I feel, the more in control I am. I want to look good for you. I want to feel like myself."

At last Marcus nodded. "I trust you, okay? I don't like it, but I trust you. If this is what you want, I'll back you up."

It was such a typical Marcus thing to say. I pulled him into a kiss. "Thank you."

With the extra weight off, I'd feel more like myself. Happier. I was sure of it.

· · · ·

Six weeks after our move east, I scheduled the surgery to have a gastric band fitted. Marcus, to his credit, was nothing but supportive, and even took the week off to help with the kids while I recovered.

Maybe I was making too much out of nothing. My family had my back. Any pressure I felt to change was in my own head, it seemed. The night before the surgery, I slept peacefully in Marcus's embrace, convinced that I'd found the solution to the source of my dissatisfaction.

Chapter Three

Once a month or so, the military wives had a get-together, which we referred to as The Coffee. In theory, The Coffee meetings were a support network for officers' wives, a chance to bond over shared experiences and exchange information on upcoming events within the community. In practice, The Coffee was a place where women went to gossip and scrutinize one another while snacking on creatively themed food and sipping cocktails or wine.

For the first few sessions of The Coffee on the new base, I hovered in the background, getting to know people. Once I had the lap band inserted and the pounds began to fall away, I felt a little more confident and outgoing. Within a few months I looked better than I had in my early years of college.

In the colder months it had made sense to dress conservatively. I decided to debut my new body during the first Coffee of late spring. New clothes. New attitude. New Amy.

• • • •

Marcus was sitting at the kitchen table reading something on his iPad when I returned from my pre-Coffee shopping trip.

"You're looking pleased," he observed. I noticed how his eyes skimmed over my body, appreciating my new shape. He would never have asked me to change, but I hadn't heard him complain about the difference in my figure.

I emptied my shopping onto the kitchen table and fished out the smart little black dress I'd just bought. I held it up so he could picture how good it would look on me, and wiggled my eyebrows.

"Cute," said Marcus warily, with the air of a man who knows nothing about clothes.

"Eight dollars at the consignment shop." I grinned. "What do you want to bet that no one notices?"

"You can buy new clothes, you know." Marcus eyed the dress again. "You don't have to get things secondhand."

I started gathering my purchases back up. "I wanted to. I like the idea of going to The Coffee and acting the part, and while everybody else is worrying about what everyone else thinks of them . . . I'll have my secret."

"Thrifty," said Marcus. "But if you want something nice, go ahead and buy it."

I sighed. "Will you hold that thought for a moment?" I disappeared into the bedroom and changed out of my sweater and jeans. The dress required different underwear so the lines wouldn't show, and a strapless bra so that the scooped collar could reveal my bare shoulders and just enough cleavage. The dress came almost to my knees, showing off the long lines of my legs without revealing too much thigh. It was tasteful, just this side of sassy, and it showed off all my best features.

I admired myself in the door-length mirror for a moment before heading back to the kitchen.

Marcus glanced up from his reading, then slowly put the iPad aside. "Amy . . ." he said, his voice low.

"Still think I need to buy new clothes to look nice?" I walked over to where he sat and leaned forward, resting my elbows on the table, giving him an excellent view of my assets.

"You look great," said Marcus, his eyes roving over me.

"What do you think? Will this be okay for tonight?" I frowned down at my bare feet. "Shoes. I forgot about shoes. Heels, do you think? Or would flats be better? I don't want to go overboard."

Marcus got up and kissed me firmly on the mouth. "I don't know about The Coffee, but I know what I think."

"Hopefully the other ladies won't have the same reaction," I teased, putting my arms around his neck and pulling him down for another kiss.

"When will Kari be here to pick you up?" he asked.

"Any minute."

Marcus ran his hands down my hips to where the dress reached my knees. "Maybe she'll be late."

"One can hope," I said, pulling on the hem of his shirt.

At that moment the doorbell rang.

Marcus groaned as I called, "Come on in."

We pulled apart as the door opened and my friend Kari walked in. She moved with the slow, loping gait of the heavily pregnant. As she rounded the corner into the kitchen, I saw her eyes bounce between me and Marcus, noting the state of my hair, his shirt untucked from the hem of his jeans, and the expressions we both wore.

"Am I interrupting something?" she asked mildly.

"Nothing much," I said. "Any chance you could leave and come back in ten minutes?"

Kari squinted at Marcus. "I can give you five."

I laughed as Marcus cleared his throat and tucked his shirt back in. "Let me grab some shoes and I'll be ready to go."

"Is that the new dress you found today?" asked Kari, checking me out. I spread my arms and rotated on the spot. She whistled. "No wonder Marcus was getting handsy. You look great. Maybe I should have gone for the surgery instead of the baby." She patted her belly. "I mean, I glow, but you're *smokin'*."

I laughed her off and ran to grab a pair of black flats from the bedroom. I could hear my best friend and my husband exchanging pleasantries in the next room, but I held back for a moment to fix my hair in the mirror. I wanted one last look at myself before I headed into the fray.

It wasn't so much that my new body had changed how I felt about my life—but it definitely changed how I felt about myself. I was in control. I was unstoppable.

I was hot again.

• • • •

Kari had been my roommate in college. She'd known me back when I was a wild child, when we'd planned to live abroad, shopping and flirting and generally rejecting society's expectations for us. She'd also seen the way Marcus had transformed me. I hadn't met up with her during the years when my family lived on O'ahu, but we'd always kept in close touch.

Kari was newly married, and her husband Raife, also active-duty army, had been assigned to the same base as Marcus shortly after we moved. I was glad to have Kari back in my life, and her presence made The Coffees much more pleasant than they might have been. I walked slowly with her as we made our way out to her car.

"My feet are so swollen," she complained. "Why didn't you warn me? I thought being a mom was about tiny outfits and stuffed animals and cuteness."

"I think you got real life confused with a diaper commercial," I said.

"That's my problem," said Kari, grinning back at me. "I always believe the ads."

Baby-glow aside, Kari was beautiful. It wasn't a polished, affected beauty achieved through makeup and expensive clothes. She was simply so earnest and pleasant that it showed on her face. It amazed me that she had married Raife—I had never thought that she would settle down, but I had never thought that I would, either. Kari lived life on her own terms, not worrying what others thought of her, and for the most part that made people like her more. I was glad that her marriage and pregnancy hadn't changed her.

Kari dragged herself into the car, then lay back against the seat with her eyes closed. "I've suffered enough, Amy," she groaned, laying her hand across her face dramatically. "Don't make me go to The Coffee. I've been good."

I straightened up in my seat, adopting the prim posture and slight drawl of most of the other women who would be in attendance. "Life is suffering. We must atone for our sins through sacrifice and boring social functions."

Kari snorted a laugh and started the car. "Don't get started now. I'll have to put up with that for the next two hours."

I slumped back against the seat and stared out the window. "It's not too late to defect. We could make a run for it."

"And do what?" Kari demanded. "I'm about to pop, and you're dressed like a call girl."

"We could rob a bank." I laughed and nudged her. "Call girl was the look I was going for, anyway. Don't be jealous."

"If you wanted to fit in you'd wear khakis and a blouse," said Kari, gesturing to her own modest outfit that clung to her pregnant belly. "So in this bank robbery scenario, am I holding the gun or taking the money? Because I'm slow, but I'm *mean*." She drew out the last word, looking back and forth from me to the road with squinted eyes. On Kari's sweet face, the expression was particularly absurd.

I worked hard to keep my mouth straight. "We could get you a pair of roller skates."

Kari hooted. "For the bank job or for The Coffee?"

"Either," I said. "Both."

"I'd steal the show."

"No, I'd just have to do something wild to upstage you."

"I would pay good money to see that. My half of the bank haul, maybe."

I patted Kari's knee. "I'm glad we live closer again."

Kari nodded. "Me too. And now, my dear . . . once more unto the breach."

We had arrived at The Coffee.

• • • •

The Coffee was held at the near-palatial home of a general. I always thought of it as the General's House, and of the hostess as the General's Wife. I didn't know her well, but everyone knew her husband—he was in charge of our husbands, and by extension his wife was in charge of us.

Among the men, an officer might openly pull rank. Among the wives, the distinctions were more subtle. The wife of such a high-ranking officer had certain social privileges that were not often extended to the other women. No one would dare snub the general's wife.

I waited for Kari at the front door, then squared my shoulders and took a deep breath before finally ringing the bell. I silently repeated the unofficial motto Kari and I had made up: *We don't have to be perfect. We just have to look that way.*

The woman who answered the door was tall, lean, and perhaps twenty years older than Kari and me. She wore her hair in a sculpted up-do, held in place with liberal applications of hairspray and decorated with a flower pin. Her navy dress was unfitted and hung shapelessly around her body. She looked more like a grandmother than Corrina ever had.

This, of course, was the general's wife.

"Kari. Amy." She nodded to each of us in turn. I saw her eyes linger on the cut of my dress, but she made no comment.

The house was packed with women. I'd met almost all of them, despite the fact that there were several times as many officers stationed on this base as there had been back on O'ahu. The problem for me wasn't matching names to faces, or even remembering personal details. The problem was that those details were almost exactly the same.

I was surrounded by Good Women, dressed in cardigans and beige slacks, whose devotion to their families stood at the heart of their conservative values. These weren't the sort of women I could be myself with, but I knew what was expected of me.

A willowy redhead named Roxanne waved me over. "Wow, Amy, you look great!"

"Thank you," I said. "Is that a new haircut?"

She touched her hair self-consciously. "It's shorter. Just a little. I wanted to try something new."

Something new? I wanted to ask her. *Next time, try something different from everyone else in this room.* Instead I said, "It looks nice."

I followed her over to a couch and sat down across from Kari.

"Cheryl's just telling me about her new homeschool group," said Kari.

"Yes," drawled Cheryl, "and I'm so glad that I found them! They hold a textbook exchange every month."

"That must be helpful," Kari said.

"It is!" Cheryl lowered her voice. "It's so hard to find good science textbooks that cover intelligent design."

Kari caught my eye and raised her eyebrows. Having Kari at The Coffee was like that—sometimes with just a look we could push our masks aside for a moment and signal to the other, *What do you say to that?*

"Have you ever thought about homeschooling, Amy?" asked Cheryl.

"Not for myself," I said. "I don't think it's my calling."

Cheryl nodded. "I just worry whether or not the children are getting a good enough education in the public schools."

"I make sure that my children have access to all kinds of education," I hedged.

Kari saved me from further conversation by pulling me aside for a moment. She had gone quite pale, and she kept rubbing her belly and shifting from foot to foot.

"Is something wrong?" I asked.

"Just my stomach. I know it's just the baby, but I'm not feeling well," said Kari, rubbing her belly. "Sorry, Amy, but I have to go."

"Do you want me to go with you?"

"You should stay." She hugged me good-bye. "I'll be fine. Call me later?"

After that, I was left to fend for myself among the other women.

• • • •

About two hours in, The Coffee began to wind down. I'd made my rounds, sipped my second glass of wine, and sampled from the sandwich tray. I'd stood my ground.

When the general arrived, the wives took this as a sign that the evening was wearing on and it was time to disappear. One by one they retreated to their cars and headed home.

"Didn't you come with Kari?" asked the general's wife, appearing at my elbow just before I left.

"I did," I admitted, impressed by her perfect memory. "I'm not far, though."

"Oh, don't be silly." She waved at her husband. "Dear?"

The general waved another cluster of ladies out on his way toward us. "How can I be of service?"

"Amy's ride left already," said his wife, patting my arm as though I were a small lost child. "Would you please see to it? Excuse me, I have some people to see off."

"It would be my pleasure to see you home," the general offered.

"Thank you," I said, dipping my head in his direction. "I don't want to trouble you. I can walk."

"No trouble at all," the general assured me. "I'm already taking Tanya May. I can drop her off and then swing past your house. It's right on the way."

My flats were comfortable enough for an indoor party, but they weren't great for walking. A ride *would* be nice. I followed Tanya and the general out to the car, and took the front seat when Tanya opted to sit in the back.

"The kids will be out of school before you know it," said the general as we drove. "Are you planning the vacation Bible school again this year?"

"Of course!" said Tanya, and she launched into a description of the theme, the guest speakers, the projects she had in mind, and so on. I stared out the window as she talked, tuning out her voice. I'd done my duty at The Coffee, and although Tanya was friendly enough, her holier-than-though attitude didn't do much for me. I was relieved when we pulled up at her house and let her out.

The general looked relieved too. "I should never have asked," he said as we waited until Tanya reached the door of her house, fumbled with the keys, and finally unlocked the door. "She's a dear woman, but I don't have much to say to her."

Although his words echoed my own thoughts, I had no interest in siding against Tanya with a man I barely knew. I settled for a curt, "Nor do I."

The general looked at me for a moment before pulling away from the curb. "Now you, Amy, you're the kind of woman a man could get to like."

I turned to face him. The general was the same age as his wife, but where his wife was stiff and matronly, the general was angular and refined. I'd never quite understood the pairing, but I'd heard stories about the general's bad behavior. He was, simply put, a rake.

"Thanks," I hazarded. The general was Marcus's superior, after all. I'd have to be careful what I said.

"You're smart, you're witty, and you're a real show-stopper." The general risked a quick glance at me to see how this was going over. *Show-stopper?* Did that line ever work?

"That's what my husband tells me," I said sweetly.

"He's a smart man."

We didn't speak again until we reached my house. I sat in the awkward silence, torn between annoyance and amusement. The general should know better than to make a pass at another man's wife, never mind the state of his own marriage. Still, the idea that I might throw over my husband for a fling with the general was laughable. For what? The attention? The draw of his rank? What on earth was supposed to be appealing about that idea?

When we pulled into the driveway, the general shut off the car. As I reached for the door handle, he turned to me.

"Well, now I know where you live. And you know where I live."

"Yes," I said awkwardly. "Thank you for the ride."

"Amy, if you ever get lonely, I want you to know that you can come to me. I know how hard it can be as an army wife." He frowned. His acting was cartoonishly bad.

I blinked at him. "I have Kari, but thank you."

He reached toward my knee, looking deadly serious. "Sometimes a man can offer help that a woman can't."

I leaned away, keeping my smile in place. "I'm very happily married, sir. Excuse me. I'm going in now."

The general jerked his hand away, and I slid out of the seat. I turned back before I closed the door.

"Oh, and sir?"

He leaned over the seat to look up at me. "Yes, Amy?"

"I think we both know that I'm out of your league."

It took every ounce of my composure for me to turn my back on the car and walk serenely to my front door, opening it without looking back.

Marcus was lounging on the couch with his iPad. He sat up when I walked through the living room.

"Well? Was it awful?" he asked.

I sat down by his feet and fixed him with a look. I was sure that the general would back off now that I'd rejected him. There was nothing Marcus could do, and he had to work with the man. There was no point in bringing it up.

"It was The Coffee," I said, and got back up. "I survived."
Kari, on the other hand, would appreciate my story. I'd call her and tell her about it, right after I changed.

Chapter Four

We were all adjusted to life on the mainland by the time I got sick.

The first morning, the kids were at school. I had eaten two pieces of toast about half an hour before, and moved on to folding laundry. I tasted bile and barely had time to rush to the bathroom before everything I'd eaten came back up.

Oh my God, I thought, bent over the toilet bowl, *I'm pregnant again.* I'd been taking birth control for years, but I knew that it sometimes failed.

I'd wait to tell Marcus, I decided. Maybe it was a stomach bug. When I didn't throw up again the next day, I took a pregnancy test. Negative. That was a relief—I loved my kids, but five was enough. Now that they were all in school, I spent most of my afternoons running them between clubs and after-school classes. I wasn't prepared to add the needs of a new baby into the mix.

A few weeks later I threw up again, this time right after lunch. I hadn't eaten anything unusual. Stress, I decided.

I was sick more and more often every passing week. I didn't have time to schedule an appointment for it, and it didn't take a medical professional to tell me what was going on. The lap band was malfunctioning. I was following all the recommendations the hospital had given me post-surgery, but now I could barely keep anything down.

My lack of free time wasn't the only thing that held me back from going to the hospital. I hated the idea of calling up Corrina and admitting that the band wasn't working out. Besides, I looked the best I ever had. I didn't want to risk going back to the way I'd looked before.

If I were just a little stronger, I told myself, I could make it work. If I were just a little tougher.

There was nothing rational about it. Corrina had told me that I would be the one to live with my choices, and if that meant I suffered for them, then I would have to accept my fate.

• • • •

"Amy, are you okay?" Marcus knocked on the bathroom door. "You've been in there for a while. Is something wrong?"

I nodded, then remembered he couldn't see me, which was just as well given that I was kneeling on the floor in front of the toilet.

"Yeah," I said aloud. "One sec."

"Sorry," he said. "I just worry." I heard his footsteps echo on the hardwood floor as he went back to bed.

In that moment, I knew that something had to change. I was either going to get this taken care of or I was going to have to explain myself when Marcus found me hunched on the bathroom floor.

I wasn't weak. That was one thing I still knew about myself. In a way, suffering made me feel strong, but if I let this go on, I was going to need serious help.

I brushed my teeth, rinsed with mouthwash so that I'd smell like peppermint rather than sickness, and went out into the bedroom.

"Sorry," I said lightly. "My stomach's bothering me."

Marcus frowned. "How long has this been going on? You've seemed . . . not yourself lately." He put his hand on my cheek and traced the lines under my eyes with his thumb. "I thought you must not be sleeping. You've been getting up a lot in the night."

"It's nothing," I lied. "I'll call to schedule an appointment right after I get the kids to school."

"Go tomorrow," he said, which was a Saturday. "I can take care of things for a few hours."

"It's not that bad," I insisted. "Maybe I'll be over it by Monday."

"If you aren't better, promise me you'll get it checked out."

I lay down in my husband's arms. How was it possible to think two opposite things at once? I wanted him to take care of me. I didn't want to admit that I couldn't take care of myself.

"I promise," I said.

• • • •

By Monday I was a wreck. My legs were shaky, my skin was clammy, and when I looked in the mirror I could tell that my eyes were too bright. I felt hot and cold by turns. Even water and warm broth turned my stomach.

The kids didn't seem to notice, except for Conrad, who was old enough to start worrying about other people. When I dropped him off at school, he hesitated before opening the door of the van.

"Are you okay, Mom?" he asked. He'd given up calling me *Mommy* at the start of the school year. Apparently it wasn't cool anymore.

"I feel a little sick today," I said. "I'm going to see if I can find someone to make it better. Don't worry about me, just have a great day at school, okay?"

"Okay." He hopped out of the van, slamming the door behind him. My word was good enough for him. Supermom had it covered.

I drove to the military hospital in a daze. I knew that I was stopping too long at lights, but my reflexes weren't up to par. I felt like I was in a dream, the kind where you need to run but your limbs won't obey you.

As I dragged myself into the ER, I wondered what this experience was supposed to teach me. To curb my pride? I tugged on my shirt, angry at this stupid band for undermining the one thing I'd done simply to please myself, the first thing in *years*. I didn't deserve this.

The nurse at the desk looked up, and I saw her eyebrows climb as she took me in. "What's wrong, honey?"

"I need to see someone," I said. My voice sounded pitiable and shaky, and I hated myself for it. "My stomach feels awful."

She nodded sympathetically and handed me a clipboard. "Fill this out, and I'll get someone to see you as soon as possible."

I filled out the paperwork, answering honestly except when it came to what was wrong with me. I couldn't bring myself to write it down, and left parts of the paperwork intentionally blank.

Good grief, Amy, this is a hospital. They're not going to judge you for having had a surgery. But I couldn't shake the feeling that getting sick was a sign of failure on my part.

They left me in the ER for half an hour. I knew that other people at nonmilitary hospitals often waited many times that long, but as

I sat there watching the clock tick away seconds, I could feel time slipping away from me. I had work to do, bills to pay, beds to make, we were looking into summer camps, and I still needed to buy groceries. We were out of detergent. I'd have to remember to pick some up on the way home.

"Amy?" Another nurse came out holding a clipboard. He motioned to me when I stood up. "We're ready for you."

I followed him down the sterile hallway. Either the lights were too bright or my eyes were having trouble adjusting. He led me to an examining room and pointed to the chair that stood in the corner. He stood by the desk, rolling the second chair back and forth without sitting down in it.

"So, Amy, what's troubling you today?" He glanced over the paperwork. "Looks like you missed a few sections here."

"Sorry, I'm not feeling well. I've been sick to my stomach a lot, and my head's . . ." I gestured as though my brains were flying away, which felt pretty much true at that moment.

He frowned sympathetically. "Poor thing. We'll get someone in here to see what's wrong."

"Could . . ." I hesitated. "Could I speak to a surgeon?"

The nurse tapped his pen on the clipboard. "Ordinarily we'd send in a GP for a stomach illness."

"I think this is a side effect from an old surgery," I said.

"Can you tell me a little more about it?"

The nurse kept looking at me, and I squirmed under his steady gaze.

"It's hard for me to talk about," I said at last. "I'd prefer to only discuss it once."

The nurse accepted this explanation without comment. "Wait right here. I'll ask the colonel to come in."

I stayed seated, looking around absently. I didn't want to read the celebrity rags that someone had stacked neatly in the magazine rack. The room was impersonal except for a few photos of children taped to the cabinet doors. Some brightly colored stick-on decals of cartoon fish had been arranged above the door, probably in an attempt to make the room a little more welcoming to children. They only drew my attention to the blankness of the other walls.

I've never liked hospitals or doctors' offices. Physicians are always trying to sell you something, and most of the time they're more interested in getting paid than in making you feel better. I folded my arms and closed my eyes, trying to block out the harsh, unnatural light from the halogen bulbs.

I jumped when the door opened and the colonel entered. The man who stepped through was tall and lean, a little older than me, with salt-and-pepper hair and a strong jawline.

"Amy?" he asked, looking up from my papers. His eyes were a startling blue, like clear morning sky or the water off the coast of O'ahu when the sun was shining.

He shook my hand and introduced himself. "I'm the head surgeon," he said. "As I understand it, you weren't exactly clear with Cecil about what brings you here." He sat down in the empty chair across from me. I examined the slope of his nose and decided that the kids in the photographs were his.

The nurse, Cecil, came in behind him, and stood watching us. I remembered someone telling me that nurses were usually expected to stay in the room during consultations, but I didn't relish the idea of telling two men about my physical problems.

"It's private," I said. "I mean, I'm not exactly comfortable talking about it."

The Doctor nodded and turned to Cecil. "Could you step out for a few minutes? I'll come get you when we're done in here."

Cecil nodded, and I was relieved when the door closed behind him.

The Doctor pushed the clipboard aside and leaned forward, resting his elbows on his knees. "Amy, I understand that discussing your health with a stranger can feel like a very personal issue. It's your body that we're talking about. But I can't help you if you won't tell me what's wrong. That's why I'm here, to fix whatever is going on. Can you trust me?"

I sat up a little straighter in surprise. There was something disarmingly sincere about the way he spoke, and the intensity in his blue eyes when he looked at me. He looked familiar, too, although I wasn't sure whether I'd run into him somewhere else or whether he reminded me of somebody famous.

"It's only private because it's embarrassing. I . . . I had a surgery, and I think something's gone wrong. I've been feeling awful lately."

"Can you be a little more specific?" he asked, sitting back and leafing through my records. "I assume you're talking about the gastric band. It looks like you had that inserted last year at a private clinic."

I nodded. "I've been throwing up."

"How often?"

"At this point, all the time. Even water."

"Ah," he said. "That's not uncommon. Sometimes the ring slips, cutting off food's pathway through the stomach, and it can result in nausea and vomiting. We can do some X-rays to be sure, but that's my educated guess."

He was so matter-of-fact. This complication was something that happened all the time, not some kind of cosmic punishment reserved for me.

"What do I do if that's the case?"

"We'll have to remove the band. It's a minor procedure, but it will completely resolve the problem."

"What about the weight?" I asked. "Won't I gain it right back?"

His eyes flickered over me, lingering on my legs and breasts for a few seconds before meeting my gaze. "You seem like an otherwise healthy woman. I'd recommend that you see a nutritionist, but I don't think that you'd need to be concerned."

I wrinkled my nose, but I nodded. "I guess we can discuss it later."

"Of course." He frowned, prodding at the chart with a long finger. "It looks like this is the first time you've come in. How long have you been having trouble with the band?"

"A few months."

He whistled. "You must be a pretty tough woman to have put up with that so long." He got up. "I'm going to send in the nurse. We'll do the X-rays right away, and we can schedule surgery if I'm right about the problem. I'll take care of you, Amy."

"Thanks," I said, and The Doctor smiled at me before he closed the door.

• • • •

During the rest of the exam, it became increasingly clear that my situation was serious. I was dehydrated despite that fact that I'd only had water for the last few days, my iron was low, my blood sugars were critical—I had been running on fumes and hadn't even registered how bad I'd let things get.

The Doctor came out to inform me that he'd been correct. The band had, indeed, slipped out of place, and he wanted to make sure I was scheduled for the next available appointment.

"I want to make sure I can be the one to operate," he said. "It won't be for two weeks, but I'll have Cecil remove the remaining fluid in the band, which should allow you to have some success with a liquid diet. We'll get you some meal-replacement shakes and supplements, and print off a list of things that you should be able to eat without making yourself sick. Hang in there for the next couple of weeks and we'll get you back to normal."

"Thanks," I said.

He scribbled his number on a slip of paper. "If you need anything, don't hesitate to call me."

I slid the paper into my purse. "I appreciate it."

"It will be okay." He held out his hand again, and I took it. I felt a prickle all down my arm as though I'd brushed my hand against a bare live wire, and The Doctor held my hand for a moment, looking me in the eyes, before he let me go.

● ● ● ●

"Did they tell you what was wrong?" Marcus asked that night.

"Complication with the band. Nothing major." I lay back in bed, exhausted. "I might take it easy for the next couple of weeks until I can get it fixed."

He nodded. "Let me know how to help you."

To his credit, Marcus didn't tell me *I told you so*, which I was sure to hear from Corrina if I ever told her what had happened. Marcus slipped into bed beside me and pulled me close, running his hand over my hair. "I'm sorry you don't feel well. I worry that you're going to blow yourself up. I see how hard you work."

I closed my eyes and let myself enjoy the sensation of his touch, intimate but not sensual. *This man really loves you*, I thought.

Still, when I turned off the light and closed my eyes, I had a sudden and vivid recollection of The Doctor's intense blue eyes.

Chapter Five

Two weeks was a long time to go without real food—I ate like a hummingbird, and my heart was always beating too fast, as if I'd run miles, even if I had only walked from the front door to the bedroom.

Still, the diagnosis helped. Instead of feeling weak, I felt like a patient. Something was wrong with me, but it was the kind of thing that could be fixed. A common surgical side effect. I wasn't special. These things just happened.

I was careful to ensure that the kids never knew anything was wrong with me. Kari and Marcus were the only ones I told about the slipped band, and I was careful to never let either of them know how bad I had really gotten. I knew how to make it look like everything was okay, even when I was falling apart. Nobody would even have guessed that I was suffering, or even that I was not feeling well.

In spite of all this, I was exhausted. Since I'd become a mother, I'd always been spread thin, but I'd always been strong enough to fix things myself, and when I fell short, Marcus was there to support me. This, however, was something that neither Marcus nor I could fix.

Thank goodness for The Doctor.

• • • •

A week into my wait, Kari delivered her baby.

Although she was my best friend, there was no way for me to drop everything and rush to her side. Besides, she had Raife, who was glued to her side for the whole labor. I had to wait until the kids went to school before I could head over to the maternity wing of the hospital and sit with Kari's mother and Raife's family, who had flown in from their home out West.

Raife's parents were excited, but from the moment I walked in, I worried that Kari's mom was going to burst a blood vessel. She looked as if she hadn't rested in days.

"Kari's going to be fine," I assured her with a hug.

"I know, I know." She sat down in a chair, then jumped up again, too anxious to settle in one place. "I mean, this is exciting, as long as nothing goes wrong, but even if it's fine it will be such a big change for all of us . . . my first grandbaby . . . didn't your mother throw a fit over your first delivery?"

I tried to imagine Corrina throwing a fit over anything. That really wasn't her style. "Not so much," I said.

"Well, all right, maybe I'm panicking." She sat down again.

I wobbled a little on my feet. I was light-headed from living on protein shakes and vitamins, and Kari's mom was taking a lot out of me. Overhead, the halogen bulbs hummed and flickered. They were giving me a headache.

"When was the last time you ate?" I asked her.

She looked at the clock, started to count back, then shrugged. "A long time."

"Why don't I get you something? A sandwich, maybe? That way you won't have to go anywhere."

"That's thoughtful, honey. I'd appreciate it."

I knew there was a cafeteria somewhere, and looking for food would be useful, as well as offering a convenient excuse for me to escape Kari's mother's nervous energy.

"I'll be back soon," I promised. On my way out, I stopped to ask Raife's parents if they needed anything.

"Just a coffee, thanks," said his mother.

A series of signs for the cafeteria led me deeper into the hospital. The halls were crowded with patients, visitors, and the hospital staff dressed either in their military uniforms or scrubs. At some point it occurred to me that I might not be able to find my way back to where I'd started, but I'd worry about that later. My friend was having a baby. I kept turning that thought over in my mind—I was happy for Kari, but a niggling worry in the back of my brain kept pushing its way through. What if motherhood changed her? What if she turned into one of the wife-clones from The Coffee, incapable of talking about anything but kids and husbands and vacation Bible school?

Come on, I told myself, *this is Kari. You went daytime skinny-dipping together during spring break in freshman year. She's not going to turn into a Stepford Wife overnight.*

Anyway, motherhood hadn't changed me that much. Had it?

I caught a whiff of bacon from the hallway ahead, and rounded the corner into the cafeteria. My stomach turned over, partly because I knew that eating anything would make me sick, but also because the food smelled great. Any food at all would have smelled great. You could have thrown a whole egg in a pan, shell and all, and it would still have gotten my mouth watering.

Rather than carry a plate of food on my way back toward the maternity ward, I opted for one of the shrink-wrapped roast beef sandwiches resting on a shelf in the cooler. I grabbed a bottle of orange juice, too, then asked for a coffee at the register.

"That's not for you, is it?" asked the man behind me.

I turned, my mouth open to answer, and found The Doctor looking over my purchase with mild horror in his eyes.

"It's for a friend," I said. "My friend's mother, that is. I'm still following the doctor's orders, if that's what you're asking."

He smiled, and it made the creases at the corners of his eyes crinkle. "I thought you were smarter than that, but you'd be amazed what people do to themselves."

I gathered everything up and stuffed the change in my purse. "I have children. Not much surprises me these days."

"I once had to remove two fishhooks from a man's thumb," he said at once. "He was trying to use the second one to get the first one out."

I snorted, then covered my mouth in embarrassment. "Wow. Okay. Surprising."

He waved the woman behind him to the register. "How are you, Amy? I hope you're hanging in there. I wish I could fit you into the schedule sooner, but . . ."

"I'm fine," I interrupted. "I mean, I will be. I'm here for my friend. She's having her first baby and her mom's kind of, well, she's being a mom, isn't she?"

"Nervous," said The Doctor, nodding. "Understandable. Do you know how to get back to maternity?"

"Eh." I pulled a face. "I wasn't really paying attention on the way here. I'll follow the signs."

"Let me walk you," he said. "I just need a coffee and a quick bite."

"Only if it's on your way."

"I can get you close," he said. "One moment."

While I waited, I closed my eyes and took a few deep breaths. The smells had left me queasy, and I longed for a time when my body would just operate smoothly, without my having to think about it so much.

"Okay." I opened my eyes to find The Doctor standing before me, a coffee in one hand, a protein bar in the other. "On to maternity."

As I glanced at the coffee cup in his hand, I caught the gold glimmer of a wedding band. Odd, he'd had pictures of his kids in the office, but none of his wife.

"I'm glad you're holding up so well," he told me as we began to walk. I could tell that he was consciously slowing his steps to match mine. On another day I would have hurried my steps to keep up with him, but I was already pushing myself.

There was no way I was going to admit that, though. "My mom didn't think I should have the surgery in the first place. I'm just getting what I deserve, right? Karma." I smiled to show that I was joking.

The Doctor frowned. "Do you believe in that? Destiny?" He didn't wait for an answer. "I don't. There are factors we can control, and there are things that happen to us. You didn't decide to let the band slip out of place, but you decided to deal with the problem. You're solution oriented. Am I right?"

I nodded. "Mostly. And no, I don't really believe in destiny."

"You don't sound sure."

"Do you usually discuss this kind of thing with your patients?"

He laughed, and I looked at him just in time to catch a glimpse of his grin. "No. But I got a feeling about you from our first meeting. You're smart, you're attractive, and you look intently at people. You're in the ninety-fifth percentile of women. Do you know what I mean? You stand out."

"Oh," I said, not sure how else to respond. It was forward, but he didn't say it in a flirtatious way. He just sounded confident. No, it was cocky. He'd labeled me, and he spoke with complete certainty, as though he were telling me something about myself that I didn't already know. Like his was the final say.

The Doctor had obviously meant to offer a compliment, but the phrasing unsettled me. It reminded me of something Marcus had said before my surgery. *You're a good-looking woman.* Good wasn't great. A ninety-five on a test was an A, but it wasn't a perfect score. What would I have to do to be in the ninety-sixth percentile? The ninety-ninth? The hundredth?

"Sorry, did I cross a line?" The Doctor asked. "I just meant that you seem like the kind of woman who wouldn't get flustered by the concept of fate. Big-picture things, anyway."

"I'm not flustered," I assured him. Not about that topic, at least. "It just seems like . . . what's the point in worrying about it? If there is no destiny, then we're talking about an arbitrary concept. If there is, we can't escape it, so why fuss? Like you said, I'm solution oriented. Talking about that won't solve anything. Next question."

"Interesting," said The Doctor, taking a sip of his coffee. "We've reached maternity."

"Ah." I peered down the hall and saw Kari's family hovering around their seats. "Thanks. I would be lost if it weren't for you." The words sounded oddly somber once they were out of my mouth.

"No problem. Best of luck to your friend. And I'll see you next week, okay? We'll get you all fixed up. Then you can have as many acidic drinks and red-meat sandwiches as you want."

I gave him a sideways smile. "Won't the nutritionist have something to say about that?"

"Such a buzzkill." He shook his head with mock solemnity. "Nice running into you."

I'd already thanked him for walking me back, so I struggled for something else to say, and before it came to me he'd turned on his heel and disappeared down the hallway.

Weird conversation, I thought, but I felt more alert than I had in days. His half-compliment nagged at me. Why did it sound like a challenge to be a better woman than I already was?

Anyway, his opinion shouldn't matter to me. He was a stranger, or close enough.

Raife appeared at the other end of the maternity hallway. His eyes were puffy and red, and he kept wiping his nose. Raife was a tough guy, not a macho type, just unshakable under most conditions. I hurried over to the family to hear what he had to say, forgetting that I was still holding a hot cup of coffee and splashing a little over the lip of the cup as I ran, scalding my fingers.

"What's happened?" Kari's mother was asking. Raife's dad rubbed his back.

"It's a girl," Raife blubbered. "It's a girl, and she's beautiful. So beautiful. She's perfect."

• • • •

My mind kept wandering back to the conversation with The Doctor. It had been a strangely personal talk, and it had the odd effect of reducing my anxiety about the upcoming operation.

"Are you worried about this surgery?" Marcus asked the night before I went in.

I shrugged, changing into a loose cotton nightdress. "Not really. I met the surgeon, and I really like him. He seems totally together. He says this is pretty routine."

"I just want you to feel better," said Marcus, opening his arms so that I could lie down beside him and let him hold me close. "We'll all be happy when you're feeling one hundred percent."

The number reminded me of the conversation I'd had with The Doctor. Marcus didn't mean quite the same thing, but the phrase made me feel better. My family was where I belonged, and we fit together. I was exactly who I needed to be.

"Marcus?"

"Hm?"

"Do you think I brought this on myself?"

Marcus hesitated, stroking my hair while he considered this. "This wouldn't have happened without the surgery, yes. Do I think you deserve this? No."

I nestled closer. "Another surgery tomorrow, then I'll be good as new. Thanks for putting up with me for the last few weeks."

He kissed my temple. "Don't apologize, Amy. You're always there when I need you. We support each other."

That was reassuring. I was lucky to have Marcus.

So why, I wondered, did I feel like there was another part of me that wanted more than his comfort? Why did part of me want him to ask what *I* thought?

Do you believe in that? Destiny?

I closed my eyes and drifted toward sleep. As soon as I felt up to it, I told myself, I would eat a steak the size of a dinner plate and chase it with a whole bottle of wine. That would help put a lot of things in perspective.

Chapter Six

The morning of my surgery, Marcus dropped me off at the hospital.

"I can shift my schedule around if you want," he said, pulling up to the main doors. "I hate just dumping you out on the curb."

"I'll be fine," I said. "They'll want to keep me overnight, and you'll have your hands full with the kids. If you're with them, I'll know I don't have to worry. I'll call tomorrow when they're ready to send me home." We could always have hired a sitter, but I didn't want Marcus to hover over me. He'd fuss, but I was used to being strong. Growing up with Corrina, I'd taught myself to be independent. I'd never learned how to let someone else take care of me. My husband understood that, and I loved him for it.

Even so, Marcus's smile was tense with worry. "Call us as soon as you're out, okay?"

I rubbed my stomach before I could stop myself. Pain radiated out from the core of me, like a spiderweb that stretched through every last nerve. My skin was tender and my mind wandered, making it difficult to keep track of conversations, even simple ones like this.

"I will. Promise."

"Amy . . ."

"You take care of our family," I said, kissing him on the cheek. "This time, I'll take care of me." I hopped out of the van before he could argue, and I hurried into the hospital.

Cecil was waiting by the front desk. He had a shadow of dark stubble along his jaw, and I wondered if he was coming off a night shift.

He looked up, and a smile tugged at the corners of his mouth. "Cute romper, and I dig the sandals," he said. "I don't think I've ever seen anyone dress up for a surgery."

I looked down at myself. "This is how I always dress."

"Most people see a surgery as an opportunity to show up in sweatpants." He picked up the clipboard with my paperwork.

"I don't own sweatpants," I said. I was torn between annoyance at his tone, and embarrassment that he was flipping through my file as we talked. I had refused to tell him what was wrong with me, but of course he had to know, especially if he was assisting in my surgery.

"Let's get you prepped, honey," said Cecil, waving me down the hall.

I settled on annoyance and followed him.

• • • •

Prepping for the removal of the band was a lot like prepping for its insertion. The main difference was how I felt. The first time around, I'd been giddy and hopeful. The second time, I was physically exhausted and emotionally drained.

"The surgeon will be in any minute," said Cecil. He hovered over the anesthesiologist, a woman who'd introduced herself as Dr. Parms and who was pointedly ignoring him. A tech stood in the corner, gloves ready, looking over my paperwork for what was probably the fifth or sixth time.

"Did you read over the pre-surgery materials?" Cecil pressed. "Do you have any questions that I can address now?"

"No. I mean, yes, I read it, but no questions."

"Any concerns?"

"No."

"If you'd like to know anything more about the procedure—"

Cecil was cut off as the door swung open and The Doctor came through. Everyone in the room shifted toward him, as if he'd altered the room's gravity for a moment simply by stepping in.

"We've gone over everything," said Cecil importantly.

"Excellent." The Doctor nodded in my direction. "Amy, I don't want you to worry about anything. You're in good hands here."

"I believe it," I answered earnestly as everyone took their places.

"Is everything ready?" The Doctor asked.

Cecil gave a sharp nod. "Yes, sir."

"Then why don't we get started?"

Dr. Parms checked her equipment, then lifted the mask and gently fitted it over my face.

"I'm going to count backward from ten," she said, her voice muffled by her own paper mask. "Ten. Nine. Eight." *Everybody is wearing masks*, I thought blearily.

After that I only heard distant mumbling, and then nothing. Numbness spread through my limbs, overriding the pain that had been my constant companion for weeks. As every muscle in my body relaxed, I looked up into The Doctor's blue eyes and let myself fall down into a dreamless chemical sleep.

• • • •

When I came to, a pleasant-looking woman was taking my pulse. She was the same build as I'd been before the band, and for a hallucinatory moment that felt like an omen.

"How are you feeling?" she asked. "You're on painkillers, but I can up the dose if you'd like."

I tried to tell her that I was fine, but the words were incoherent in my mouth.

She nodded sympathetically. "If you need anything, press this button, okay?" She pointed to a red button not far from my left hand. "Someone will be right here to help you with anything you need."

"Careful, Barb. She's the kind of patient who says the pain's a four when it's a ten."

We both turned to see The Doctor leaning against the door of my room. My eyes widened in surprise—he wasn't wearing his usual white coat or pristine scrubs. He'd changed into dark jeans and a navy blue polo that made his eyes stand out more than usual. He gave me a warm smile.

"How are you, Amy?"

"Okay," I managed to say. The more I woke up, the more my body seemed willing to obey me. I hurt, but it was a different kind of hurt. Centralized, not expansive.

"Didn't I promise you would be?"

The nurse, Barb, pointed at the button again. "I get that you're a tough one, but you don't have to impress anyone, Amy. Let me know if you need anything. I'll come running." She dipped her head to The Doctor and went out into the hall.

The Doctor pulled a chair up next to my bed. "Will someone be here for you tonight?" he asked.

"Tomorrow. Marcus has his hands full with the kids," I said, forgetting that The Doctor and my husband had never met. I swallowed. My mouth was dry. I should have thought to ask Barb for some water.

As if he could read my mind, The Doctor went to the little sink in the corner of the room and ran me a cup of water before sitting down. "I get the impression that you're the kind of woman who likes to do things her own way, but I have some suggestions for how to speed up your recovery, and I hope that you'll try to follow them."

I nodded meekly, sipping my water.

"It's important to eat a lot of protein right now," he said. "After surgery, your body needs a lot of support, especially given the state you were in. I'd like you to meet with a nutritionist, but in the meantime, I recommend a lot of fresh fruits and vegetables, and drink plenty of fluids."

"Yes, sir," I said, putting my empty paper cup aside. "I'll be good."

"Excellent." He gave me a secretive smile. "But sometimes it's okay to treat yourself." He reached into the pocket of his coat and produced two small cups of chocolate pudding. "Here. A reward for making it through the last few weeks."

The painkillers meant that I was mostly numb, but when I saw those pudding cups I was suddenly aware that I had been basically starving for weeks.

"Can I eat those now?" I asked skeptically.

"No solids, no acid, no carbonation . . ." He ticked the merits of pudding off on his fingers.

Most days I would have turned my nose up at pudding, but at that moment, it seemed like The Doctor had offered me two little cups of heaven. I opened the lid of the first one and took a plastic spoonful. I stifled a groan. Nothing had ever tasted better. I resisted the urge to shovel it into my mouth and took small bites, savoring my ability to eat without worrying I'd throw up in an hour.

"Thank you," I said, scraping the cup clean.

He watched me eat, a slow smile spreading across his face. It was different than the smiles he'd given me before. Those smiles were mechanical, practiced expressions meant to put patients at ease. This smile was unconscious and genuine.

"What?" I opened the second cup.

"You're just . . ." He seemed to catch himself. "I'm just glad you're feeling better."

"Me too," I said. "I'm very grateful."

"I hope you'll follow up with a specialist. There's a panel on nutrition later this week. Most people considering serious weight loss have to go through a process before they qualify for surgery. I think it would give you some ideas for how to move forward. Will you come?"

I considered this, sucking on the spoon. "I'm very busy," I said at last. "I have a lot to catch up on."

"I insist," said The Doctor firmly. "You need to take care of yourself. I'm sure you've got a lot on your plate, but your health should come first."

I sighed. He was back in the role of head surgeon. "Okay, okay. I promise I'll come."

"I'll make sure that someone gives you the details." The Doctor stood up, pulling on his jacket. "I should go. My kids are waiting on dinner."

The pudding was gone, and I lay back in my bed, already drowsy again. Probably on account of the medication, I guessed.

"Go home, feed your kids, and come back," I murmured. "Next time, bring some vanilla, too."

He laughed. "You'll be fine here, I promise. If they need me, I only live a few blocks away. The nurses will take care of you."

"I want *you* to take care of me," I told him, bleary again from the painkillers.

If he answered me, I didn't hear it. I was already asleep.

• • • •

By the time Marcus came to pick me up the next morning, I would have eaten anything he put in front of me.

"How are you feeling?" he asked as I slid into the van beside him.

"Great. Can we swing by a drive-through and get, like, fifty cheese-burgers?"

Marcus laughed in surprise. "Burgers? Who are you and what have you done with my wife?"

"I'm the ravenous ten-foot lizard left in her place post-surgery," I said. I began to sort through all the instructions they'd handed me at the desk. Among my discharge papers was a scrawling, handwritten note that gave the time and date of the nutrition panel The Doctor had mentioned.

"Do you really want to grab something now?" asked Marcus, changing lanes to bring us closer to a fast food joint.

I held the piece of paper and sighed. "No, I should take it easy for the day. I'll have to watch what I eat."

"Is this about how you look?" asked Marcus warily.

I shook my head. "This is because my stomach's had a rough time lately."

"Okay." A pause. "I'm glad you're feeling better."

"Me too." I slipped the paper back into the stack of instructions and pamphlets. "But I'm going to have to go in for some follow-up stuff. They want me to see a nutritionist."

"Sounds reasonable. Take all the time you need. It would be good for you to get out more."

I shifted in my seat to watch my husband as he drove. "Do you think I'm turning into a shut-in?"

"Our kids have lives now," said Marcus, setting a hand on my knee for a moment without taking his eyes off the road. "You could have a life too, you know? Outside of the house? You've been such a great mom, but I'd love to support you in finding your own thing now. Does that sound crappy? Like I don't respect what you do?"

"No," I said, thinking it over. "No, it doesn't. You might be right. Let me get this under control and then I'll think about it."

"Take your time. I just want you to be happy."

I was already happy. Wasn't I?

• • • •

Three days later, when I stepped into the room where the nutritional panel was scheduled, I felt instantly out of place.

Some of the other attendees were candidates for the same surgery I'd gone through. Unlike me, however, most of the other patients were at the beginning of their weight-loss program. From the moment I stepped in the door, I was aware of people looking at me from the corners of their eyes. *What's she doing here?* I was sure they were asking themselves.

Oh, get over yourself, nobody cares what you're up to. I took a seat at the back of the room, crossed my legs, and waited for the speakers to arrive.

When thirty or forty people had taken their seats, Cecil stepped to the front of the room.

"Hello," he said loudly, tapping the microphone next to the speakers' podium. "Can everybody hear me?"

Several members of the audience murmured an unenthusiastic response.

"Excellent." Cecil folded his hands on the podium and looked around at all of us. He planted his feet in what was probably supposed to be a power stance. "Just a few things before we get started. I will be your moderator today. All of your questions will need to come through me. Please don't interrupt; we have a schedule to keep and there will be time at the end to ask any questions specific to your circumstances."

I rolled my eyes slowly toward the ceiling.

"Let's get started. Our first speaker, Doctor Chien, will be discussing the physical therapy options that we offer here."

Cecil scooted out from behind the podium and found a seat in the front row. A woman about my age took his place.

I tuned out as she talked about the various programs available for patients interested in PT, and found myself looking around at the other members of the audience. I hated talking about weight, especially my weight, and I certainly didn't want to be part of this crowd. It wasn't that I felt particularly put off by this group of people, mostly much older and much heavier than I was. I wished them luck in their search for better health. I just hated wasting my time, and I didn't belong there. I had plenty to get done at home. Sitting in the uncomfortable plastic hospital chair wasn't accomplishing anything. I could sneak out the back door, I reasoned. But when I looked up, I saw The Doctor sitting against the front wall.

He'd worn his uniform for the seminar. It was the first time I'd seen him working in his military fatigues rather than his usual scrubs and coat.

As if he could feel my gaze, The Doctor turned his head and caught my eye. He nodded his head slightly without breaking eye contact. I nodded back. *Okay. I'm here.*

I expected him to turn back to the speaker, but he held my gaze for a long moment. The hospital chair was uncomfortable. I wanted to move, but I didn't want to be the one to look away first.

After what felt like a very long time, his mouth quirked up in a subtle smile and he turned back to the therapist, who was wrapping up her speech.

Cecil leapt to the podium and leaned toward the microphone. "Does anyone have any questions?"

I did. I had a lot of questions. Just none for the physical therapist.

I kept looking around the room during the follow-up questions, and then during the nutritionist's talk. I couldn't seem to focus. Now and then my gaze slid back toward The Doctor, but he was never looking my way.

The nutritionist took questions through Cecil, and then Cecil introduced The Doctor. He stood up slowly, ambled to the podium as if he had all the time in the world, and spent a long moment adjusting the height of the microphone. When that was done, he rolled his shoulders, looked around at the audience, and finally began to speak.

"Some people see surgery as a quick fix. A magic pill, if you like. It sounds easier than long-term dietary management. Let me assure you, this is not the case. A successful surgery relies as much on a patient's dedication to the process as the surgeon's technical skill. There can be painful side effects, as some of you already know." His eyes found me. "Surgery isn't an instant solution. The result can be significant, but the risks can be significant as well, especially when a patient fails to keep track of his or her own progress."

He was proud of his profession, that was obvious, and evidently he was tired of people making excuses about why they couldn't be responsible for themselves.

I watched him closely, trying to follow the thread of his talk, but there was something distractingly familiar in his confident tone and, yes, arrogance. He was exactly the type of man I'd been drawn to before I met Marcus.

What did it mean that I found myself attracted to him? Nothing. I'd see him a few more times in a professional setting and then I'd move on with my life.

He took a few questions at the end of his talk, which was the final segment of the panel. I didn't raise my hand. When he returned to his chair and Cecil thanked us for our time, I hung back with a cluster of other patients. All of us wanted a private word with the speakers, although I wasn't sure I had concerns, exactly. I just wanted to talk to The Doctor, to see how this newfound knowledge of my attraction to him held up in conversation.

When he saw me, The Doctor tapped the nutritionist on the shoulder and directed her attention to me. "This is Amy. I mentioned her earlier, remember? She was just in for surgery, but she's looking for some long-term nutrition advice. She'd like to get into your calendar." I shrank from this public announcement of my surgery, even if the public in question consisted of seven strangers and three people who already knew why I was there.

The brunette shook my hand. "Sure thing, Amy. Great to meet you. Here's my card. Call in to schedule an appointment and we'll see what we can work out, okay?"

"Okay," I said, trying not to let my skepticism show. I slid the card into my purse. She seemed nice enough, but I still wasn't sure about the idea of seeing her on a regular basis. Nutrition was a soft science, and I had no interest in fad diets.

"Great. Do you have any questions about the presentation?" She gave me a wide and earnest smile.

I didn't think I'd heard two full sentences of her talk. "Not at the moment," I said.

"Wonderful. I look forward to seeing more of you." She shook my hand and turned to the next patient who had questions about his per-surgery diet restrictions.

"Glad you could make it," said The Doctor softly. He held my gaze for another moment, giving me that same intense and searching look before shaking my hand too, and waving me out the door.

Chapter Seven

"Marcus?" I called as I walked into the kitchen. "Oh, good. You're still home."

"I've got another few minutes before I have to go." He looked up from his half-packed lunchbox. "What's up?"

"Remember when you said that you thought I should get out more? What did you have in mind?"

Marcus cocked his head, looking across the room at me in an attempt to gauge my mood. "Just that you deserve to spend more time on yourself. Why?"

I prodded the screen of my tablet with one thumb, scrolling up and down through a website I'd visited a dozen times in the last week. "I was thinking about going back to school."

Marcus walked over to me and leaned back against the counter. "What for? Subject, I mean."

"I was thinking about going into counseling."

"You were psych in college, right?" He bumped me affectionately with his shoulder. "If that's what you want, I think you should go for it."

"Just like that? You don't want to talk about how this would impact our family, our finances, our . . ." I gestured to indicate the house. "Our lives?"

"Amy." He took my hands in his. "I trust you. You've been in charge of raising the kids, you've been in charge of our finances, you've been in charge of . . ." He imitated my all-encompassing gesture. "If you decide that you want to go back to school, then I know it's the right choice."

I squeezed his hands. "That means a lot."

He kissed my cheek, then looked at his watch. "I should get going. Let me know what you decide and we'll talk about logistics, okay?"

I thumbed through the website again. It felt as though I'd decided before I'd even thought to ask the question.

• • • •

"You're healing up nicely," The Doctor told me. Cecil hovered over his shoulder, scanning his notes and nodding from time to time. The Doctor spun his chair slightly to move away from the nurse's scrutiny. "I only have one concern, and that might require a follow-up with a specialist."

"I feel fine," I said.

The Doctor looked down his nose at me. "Amy, from what I know, you'd say you felt fine even if both your legs were broken and your hair was on fire. Even if you really *do* feel okay, that doesn't mean we shouldn't take precautions."

"An ounce of prevention is worth a pound of cure," said Cecil wisely from above. I was sure that I saw The Doctor's eye twitch slightly.

"When your band was first fitted, it attached at the top part of your stomach to help you feel full sooner. When it slipped, it hourglassed your stomach, meaning that food could get partway in before your body rejected it. When your food came back up, it was accompanied by a great deal of stomach acid. That acid might have permanently damaged your esophagus."

"Wouldn't I have a sore throat or something?" I asked, unable to stop myself before I reached up to touch my neck, as if I would be able to feel the acid burns from the outside. "Really, I don't notice any pain like that. I promise."

"Just because you don't have any symptoms now doesn't mean that there won't be complications down the line." He leaned back in his chair and crossed his legs, tapping my file on one knee. I felt as though I were a child receiving a dressing-down after bringing home a bad report card.

I met his eyes. It was amazing how long he could go without blinking. For a few seconds we stared at each other, me with my eyes narrowed. The Doctor was just amused enough that it quirked the corners of his mouth up into a little crescent moon of a smile. I remembered his fervor at the panel, the way he'd derided patients who didn't advocate for themselves.

"I'll do the follow-up," I said at last. "But please, no more seminars."

"And the nutritionist?"

"I'll give her a try, but if I don't think it's helping, I'll stop."

Cecil shook his head sadly as if I were a personal disappointment. The Doctor swiveled his chair again. Marcus would have said that I was being reasonable and that he trusted my judgment, but The Doctor shook his head. "I want you to keep at least three appointments."

"Two," I said. "I'll know how I feel in two."

The Doctor's mouth quirked up again and he shook my hand. "Fair enough. Let me know how the follow-up goes. I'd like to schedule one more appointment with you beyond that, just to be sure everything's healing correctly."

"I'll get you the number," said Cecil. "And I'll see about putting you in the calendar."

I liked the idea of getting this over with, of putting the whole thing behind me. Still, the thought of scheduling my final exam with The Doctor left me with an odd feeling of disappointment. The sensation of something left unfinished.

• • • •

I finished my application for the counseling program the day before my appointment with the throat specialist.

"Is this even a good idea?" I asked Marcus for what was probably the millionth time. I wanted him to give me answers, to check me if I was being selfish. He'd warned me against the stomach band, and he'd been right about that.

"It's your life," said Marcus. "What do you want from your life?"

I'd wanted to be a good mother and a good wife. Somehow, applying to school felt like I was replacing my other callings, rather than supplementing them.

"Are you afraid?" asked Marcus.

I blinked at him. "What, that I won't get in?"

"I don't know. You just seem . . . tense. Anxious."

I picked at the seam of the couch cushion. "Maybe I'm scared that if I make a big change, then I won't know who I am anymore."

"I know who you are," said Marcus. He scooted closer and put his arm around me. "You're strong. You're independent. You're smart. You won't lose those things. What you're doing will change. That's all."

I leaned to the side until my head rested on his shoulder. "I don't know why I feel so conflicted about this."

"Change is hard."

I lifted my head to look at him. "Are you afraid?"

He laughed and pulled me closer. "Of what?"

"That I'll get my own life. That I won't be around as much. That we'll drift apart and our marriage will implode."

"The first two are fine with me. The last one, not so much. Can we skip that step?"

"Oh, fine." I sighed. "Since you asked nicely."

He kissed me on the temple. "Let's give it a shot. I'm always willing to take a risk if it means you'll be happy."

I squeezed his hand. Then I picked up my laptop, opened the page with my application, and clicked *Send*.

• • • •

The esophageal specialist, Dr. Randall, was a friendly middle-aged man with tidy black hair and a pleasant demeanor that, as far as I could tell, had been honed into automatic dialogue by his years in the profession.

"How are you feeling?" he asked, sitting down across from me.

"Fine."

"I'm glad to hear it," he said, but only in passing. I was certain that if I'd said the opposite, he'd have responded, *I'm sorry to hear it*, and moved along to his next line anyway. His tech, a young woman, nodded along with everything he said.

"Here's the routine. We're going to have you sit back on the table, and we're going to insert a tube through your nose. At the end of this tube is a tiny camera, and we'll be able to see everything it sees inside you on that screen there." He pointed to a monitor. "I realize that this sounds pretty unpleasant, but we do this kind of exam all the time. There's no pain, and no reason to be concerned."

I felt like I was reading a hospital pamphlet, one written for dummies that didn't include technical terms like *endoscopy* or, even worse, *transnasal esophagoscopy.*

Dr. Randall patted his knees. "Any questions?"

I shook my head. In a way, his sterile, rote monologue was comforting. This wasn't personal, and by now his exam required more muscle memory than actual focus.

"Good, good. You'll be mostly upright the whole time, and I'm sure you'll be glad to hear that you won't need to change into a paper robe." He laughed mechanically. He must have laughed at the same joke thousands of times.

I was about to get up and move to the exam table when there was a knock at the door. I dropped back into my seat. Someone must need Dr. Randall or have a pressing question about another patient. I didn't mind waiting. The idea of having a tube fed through my nostrils wasn't exactly thrilling.

When the door opened, however, I recognized the man on the other side. It was The Doctor.

"Hello, Amy," he said, stepping into the room. He was dressed in his military uniform again, looking as crisp as he had in the seminar. I frowned in confusion—there was no good reason for him to show up to this appointment at all.

"Hello, sir," said Dr. Randall stiffly. Apparently he hadn't asked The Doctor to attend. How had he even found out when my appointment was scheduled?

"You don't mind if I stay for the exam, do you, Amy?" he asked. "I just wanted to make sure you're in the clear."

I looked to Dr. Randall, who didn't seem to find this out of the ordinary. "Why not?"

The Doctor sat down in Dr. Randall's chair and folded his hands in his lap. After a moment's uncertainty, I decided to pick up where we'd left off and moved onto the exam table. I'd worn a knee-length fitted skirt that day, and I pressed my knees together as I sat back, wishing I'd chosen jeans instead.

"All right, let's get started," said Dr. Randall. He and the tech prepared the camera, speaking to each other in curt phrases as they made sure everything was in working order. This gave me a moment to raise my eyebrows significantly at The Doctor, who responded with a cool nod of his head.

"We're going to use a little local anesthetic," said Dr. Randall. "The gel will numb everything and you'll feel almost nothing during the procedure, but if you can relax, too, that will be a big help."

The tech sponged a blue gel around my nostrils. "I know this feels weird," she said apologetically.

All this time, The Doctor was watching me.

Within seconds, my face lost feeling. It was a strange sensation, as if part of me had simply vanished. I was strongly aware of the not-feeling, and I felt an urge to reach up and trace the contours of my own face, to ensure that it was still there. My arms actually jerked in anticipation of the movement before I told myself that I was being foolish.

"Here we go," said Dr. Randall, brandishing a thin coil of flexible tubing. Skinny it may be, but I didn't like the look of it. Dr. Randall and his assistant fed the tube through my nose, and I did my best to feel calm and relaxed. Years of being a military wife had taught me to *look* calm and relaxed, which was not the same thing.

"Okay, lights off," said Dr. Randall, turning to look at the computer.

"I can get it," said The Doctor, and he reached out one long arm to flip the switch. Then the four of us were in the dark, watching a live feed of my esophagus on the computer screens.

I wished that The Doctor hadn't come. Not that it mattered—he'd operated on me only a few weeks before, and surely that hadn't been a flattering sight. Still, it was different, with him looking so crisp and neat, and me tipped backward on a table with two people eagerly stuffing medical equipment down my nose.

"Looking good," said Dr. Randall. "I don't see anything to worry about."

I gave a halfhearted thumbs-up.

I risked a glance down at The Doctor, and by the light of the screens I could barely make out his expression. He smiled at me and leaned forward in the chair, putting his hand on my calf.

My breath caught in my throat, and not just because of the camera tubing. He rubbed his hand over my knee and onto my lower thigh. The touch lasted only a few seconds, and neither the tech nor Dr. Randall even realized it had happened. They were too busy examining my insides to have any idea what was going on in the room.

There was nothing inherently suggestive about The Doctor's caress, but it crossed a line. Until that moment we'd always been friendly but relatively formal with each other. There was nothing formal about his touch. The warmth of his hand went right through me and left my skin tingling, my breathing erratic.

"Are you okay?" asked the tech sympathetically, feeding the last of the tubing back out. "I know it feels totally weird, but we're done now. It looks like you're good to go."

The Doctor turned the light back on, and the sudden brightness of the room made me flinch. There had been a surreal quality to that moment in the dark, a sensuality that couldn't survive the yellow flicker of the halogen bulbs.

"No acid burns at all," added Dr. Randall with a fatherly smile. "You're good as new."

"Thanks," I said, my nose raw from the tubing, my cheeks warm from the exchange they hadn't seen. "I'm glad to hear it. I felt fine." I tried to give The Doctor a smug look to remind him that I'd been right, but I couldn't keep eye contact with him.

"We'll get you out of here, then," said Dr. Randall. He shook hands with me, then with The Doctor.

"I'll get you a glass of water," said the tech, reaching over to the sink. "It helps, I promise."

On his way out, The Doctor gave me another of his lingering glances, and although I tried, I couldn't bring myself to meet his gaze.

He knew the effect his touch had on me, and he also knew that I was okay with it.

• • • •

Marcus got home after dinner. The kids were already bathed and sprawled on the floor of the family room watching TV. I met him at the door with a kiss, then held tightly to him, running my hands over the back of his neck and through the stubble of his close-cropped hair.

"This is nice," he said, coming up for air. "What did I do to deserve such a warm welcome?"

"I was thinking about you all day," I said, which was mostly true. My body was still on fire from that brief touch, and rather than linger on the moment, I wanted to channel my desire toward Marcus. Wasn't that right? Wasn't it a good thing to have every desire come back to him? Wasn't that the sign of a strong marriage?

"Do we have any time?" he asked, looking around in search of the children.

"What if I said no?"

"I'd say give me five minutes," he said, untucking my shirt.

"What if I said yes?"

He raised an eyebrow wickedly. "Even better."

It wasn't wrong to want what wasn't mine, so long as I stayed true to what was. I'd been a wild girl, and Marcus had tamed me. This was the proof.

Chapter Eight

"Oh my God." Kari flopped down on the bench beside me. Her month-old baby, Yasmine, wriggled in the sling across her chest. Kari let her head roll back and slumped against the wooden bench with a groan.

"You're posture's gone down the toilet," I smirked.

"I thought it was a pain walking around with this thing in my belly. Now she's on the outside and she's even *heavier*. You didn't warm me about this. You were supposed to warn me."

"'This thing' is your darling, precious daughter." I leaned over Yasmine, making kissy faces at her and gently pinching her fat cheeks. "Just think, in a few years this sweet angel will be old enough to attend Tanya May's vacation Bible school!"

Kari let out a snort of laughter. "Is she too young to start home-schooling?"

"Kari," I said seriously, "they are never too young."

"The baby's here!" cried Margie, reaching the highest point on the slide and staring down at us, her eyes growing wide. "The baby!" She flung herself onto the plastic tunnel and came tumbling out the bottom a few seconds later. Lydia shrieked and ran after her. The twins heard this news from their seats on the see-saw and abandoned their game to investigate. Conrad, who already had four little sisters, gave up his swing reluctantly and followed last.

"What's the big deal with babies?" he asked morosely, hands stuffed deep in his pockets. "Why do girls go crazy for them?"

Lydia ignored him. "Can I hold her?"

I saw Kari's hesitation.

"She's still very small," I said. "Maybe another time."

Lydia groaned, but Kari shook her head. "It's okay. I'm overprotective. Just make sure to support her head. She's too young to do it on her own."

Lydia accepted Yasmine gently. Margie cooed, letting the baby grab her fingers, and the twins tickled her until I could see that Kari was getting anxious and I had to tell my kids to give their new friend back to her mom.

"Did you hear?" asked Lydia once Yasmine was safely back in hand. "Mommy's going to school."

"School?" asked Margie, looking up at me. "What are you gonna do there?"

"Take classes, dummy," said Conrad.

I said, "Be nice to your sister," and raised my eyebrows in warning.

"School?" asked the twins, pulling faces at each other. "School?" They found this, for whatever reason, terribly funny, and began to laugh at each other behind their hands.

"Do you mean you'll be working on a degree?" asked Kari in surprise. "I thought you had your hands full."

"I do." I looked at my kids. Conrad was already wandering back to the swing set, and Eliza and Alice had started a game that involved throwing pieces of the orange-tinted playground mulch back and forth. "I'm just starting to feel a little . . . stuck, you know? I want to have a career someday. I don't want to be like some wives who spend their whole lives killing time."

"I think it's wonderful," said Kari, rocking a sleepy Yasmine in her arms. "You're going to be great, Ames."

"Thanks," I said, and I bumped her shoulder with mine. "You're the best."

"You say that now," said Kari.

"I'll say it always," I assured her.

• • • •

As I'd promised, I scheduled an appointment with the hospital's nutritionist.

"I'm glad you came, Amy," she said, smiling warmly and shaking my hand. "We met at the panel, didn't we? I'm Dr. Lyons, but you can call me Joan. I know you've had some complications with surgery, but now that you're starting with a healthy weight, you're in great shape to move forward."

"Thanks," I said, fidgeting uncomfortably in my chair. I hated talking about my weight with strangers. I hated thinking of my body as something that I had to *manage*.

Dr. Lyons—Joan—reached for a stack of charts. "You might be familiar with the old food pyramid. The Center for Nutrition put out an updated chart a few years ago. It's not perfect, but it's a decent model for getting us to think about how we eat."

It was all I could do not to groan. Give me fifteen minutes and Internet access, and I could find any of this information myself. Most of it was common sense: eat less and move more.

I nodded and made interested noises through the rest of the appointment, pretty much the way I would have done at a Coffee. For the most part I was tuned out, repeating to myself, *This is a waste of time, this is a waste of time*, in internal monotone.

When our half hour was up, Joan asked me when I wanted to schedule another appointment.

"I'll have to call when I'm in front of my calendar," I told her. She was so genuinely nice, I didn't have the heart to tell her that I was never coming back.

• • • •

The only graduate program I'd applied to had a campus twenty minutes away from our house. As much as I enjoyed the idea of transforming into a freer and more empowered version of myself, someone the younger me could have respected, I couldn't justify a longer commute. I might have felt differently if I knew exactly what I wanted out of the program, but the only thing I felt sure of was that I needed a change. I'd been a mom for a third of my life, but my kids were growing up.

I'd turned my application in to the program at the beginning of the summer. They accepted me for the following spring, but a few days later I received a follow-up email saying that due to a few students turning down offers, I would be eligible to start that fall.

That night, I found Marcus on the back porch. He was sitting on one of the Adirondack chairs, legs stretched out in front of him, staring out into the night.

"Mind if I join you?" I asked.

He jumped as if I'd startled him, then motioned to the other chair.

"What's on your mind?"

"You looked like you were the one doing some heavy thinking," I said, settling in. "I wanted to talk to you about school. It sounds like I'll be able to start at the end of the summer."

"Already?" Marcus smiled. "That's great."

"Don't you think it's happening a little fast?" I asked. "What exactly am I supposed to do?"

"Leap in feet first," he said easily.

"Are you sure? You're not worried?"

"That's what we did."

I hesitated, then reached for his hand, because of course he was right. I'd fallen for him so fast, even though I'd never have guessed he would be my type. Motherhood was about mitigating risk. If I was going to make a change, maybe taking a risk or two would be a good way to start.

"You're right," I told him. "I'll accept and see how it goes."

Marcus nodded, but there was something odd in his expression.

"Penny for your thoughts?"

He rubbed his chin. "I got some news today, too."

"Hm?"

"I'll be deployed again starting in the fall."

I tightened my grip on his hand. "So soon."

"It's what they moved me out here for. I was handpicked for this mission. It will be good for my career."

"I'm sure it will," I said.

"Aw, Amy." Marcus shifted in his chair so that he faced me. "I'm sorry. The timing is horrible. They just debriefed us today."

I leaned my head back and closed my eyes. "I know that you don't have any control over this."

Marcus squeezed my hand. "But listen, you're going to be fine. You'll start your classes, you'll have a couple of months to get in the groove, and I'll be back before your first year is over."

I swallowed. "One year?"

"Less. Not even nine months."

Toughen up, Amy, I told myself. *You're getting soft. You've done this before.* I leaned over the arm of my chair to kiss his cheek.

"I'm not worried. You'll be okay, and so will we."

"That's my girl," said Marcus with a bemused smile.

We sat there for a while, not talking, just breathing the cool night air and listening to the buzz of insects. Above us, the light in Conrad's room went dark, and we were alone in the world for a little while.

I wondered whether he would have thought more of me, or less, if I'd cried.

• • • •

"How was your meeting with the nutritionist?" The Doctor asked.

I shook my head. "I know I promised you two visits, but she didn't tell me a single thing I didn't know already. It felt like she was reciting a Wikipedia article."

"She's a wonderful nutritionist," said The Doctor, but I caught his smirk before he could hide it. "She's genuinely concerned about the welfare of each patient in her care."

"Everything she said was common-sense stuff. Eat more kale, eat less sugar. I get it. I know what to do. I'm doing it. It's working." The Doctor ran a hand through his salt-and-pepper hair. "I'd like to see you keep up with this portion of the program. When people strike out on their own too early in the process, they tend to go off-track."

I leaned in close. "Can't I just come check in with you instead?"

He opened his mouth, then closed it again.

"I know you're not a nutritionist. I know it's not in the job description. But I also know what I see. You're telling me that Dr. Lyons, I mean Joan, cares about every one of her patients, but she could have been talking to *anyone* during our appointment. It was all rote. It's different with you. You're personal. You . . . care."

The Doctor swallowed. I was strangely pleased with myself for unsettling him. He'd thrown me for a loop a few times—it was nice to be the person with sure footing for once.

"You're the one who wants me to do this, aren't you?" I coaxed.

He nodded once, firmly. "Okay. I'd like to start by asking you to keep a food diary. That way I can see your baseline and tailor your habits from there."

"Sounds reasonable."

"Reasonable is good." The Doctor looked at his watch. "I should warn you, Cecil will be stopping by soon to get me. I have a surgery scheduled at two o'clock." He was wearing his formal expression again, the one that put me at arm's length. I suddenly remembered my thought from just before the surgery, right before I went under his knife: *We are all wearing masks.* I wanted to find a way to soften that stiff expression.

"I did have one question," I said.

"Ask away."

"Tell me about the other day. In Dr. Randall's office."

He met my eyes with that deep, intent look that was already becoming familiar. I remembered the warmth of his hand on my leg, the thrill his touch had sent all through my body, and the blood rushed to my face again. This time, though, I held his gaze.

"That was not a professional gesture," he admitted.

"What was it?"

The Doctor's lips quirked up in smile that promised trouble. "Opportunistic, I'm afraid."

"But not impulsive."

"On the contrary, the maneuver was thoroughly considered prior to execution."

I bit back a laugh. I wasn't sure I wanted to discourage him, but I didn't want to encourage too much.

Cecil poked his head into the room, looking back and forth between the two of us with a frown and saving me from having to come up with a witty retort.

"Your two o'clock is finishing up the paperwork and will be ready in five. I'm going to wash up and met you there. Unless you're busy?"

"We're just finishing now," said The Doctor easily, as if there was nothing odd going on. His casual tone was almost enough to convince me that there was nothing unusual about the head surgeon advising a patient on her diet plan. Cecil backed out of the room without a word.

"So, lots of protein, small but regular meals, and limit your sugar intake as much as possible." The Doctor reached out to shake my hand, as if we'd been talking about food the whole time. "Keep a detailed food journal and I'll see you in a week."

I took his hand, and that electric jolt of warmth passed through me again. "Next week," I agreed.

He led me out the door, then headed down the hallway in the opposite direction from where I was going, looking back once to wave before he turned a corner and disappeared.

He could have given me a book to read. A blog to follow. There was no need for us to make another appointment so soon, but on my way out I scheduled one anyway.

• • • •

I'd been excited about the idea of starting classes. Apparently, in the thrill of making big decisions and choosing a career path, I'd forgotten that my classes would be populated with other students.

Many of those students were fresh out of college. I'd spent most of a decade raising a family and running a home, and while that gave me the advantage of perspective that a lot of the younger students seemed to lack, it also meant that they had never left academia. Sitting for classes, taking notes, making time for homework, and everything else that came with formal schooling was second nature to them. I had to learn it all over again.

"It's like having baby brain," I told Kari. "I can't seem to keep track of things. Then I come home from cramming all this stuff into my brain, and I still have my life."

"I've seen you in action, Ames," said Kari, bouncing Yasmine on her knee. "You're supermom, right? Adding more to your workload only increases your heroic powers."

"I'm not sure it's true, but thanks for saying it." I hesitated. "I'm just trying to figure out how to balance everything—home, school, my nutrition appointments . . ."

"Good grief," said Kari, looking up from her baby in surprise, "are they still making you go to those things?"

For a moment I debated explaining everything to her. Kari knew more about me than nearly anyone alive, and I'd never been able to keep a secret from her. I'd never tried. But what would I say? *I think I'm falling for my surgeon?* Hardly. There wasn't anything to tell. We'd scheduled more meetings than were necessary and sometimes flirted. Really, I didn't know how to explain what was happening.

So instead, I bit my tongue and resolved not to mention the meetings to Kari again. The truth was that I felt just as out of place in my classes as I had at the hospital's weight loss panel, while a man who should have been a stranger was becoming one of the most significant people in my life.

"It's just for a little while," I told her. "They just want to make sure I'm okay."

Not long ago, Kari would have sniffed out the fact that something was off. Today she just said, "I hope you are too," and didn't ask another question.

• • • •

I checked my watch for the fourth time. The Doctor had never been late before. I was always on time; he was always early. But now he was almost fifteen minutes late, which in any other doctor's office would have been no big deal.

It felt like a big deal.

You're making too much out of it, I told myself. I folded my hands in my lap, hiding my watch from sight. I didn't want to worry. I didn't want to think about time. Appointments with The Doctor were something I looked forward to, despite how little sense that made when I looked at it too closely.

I should go.

I didn't want to go.

Really, though, why was I here? He was busy. I was wasting his time. I was wasting my time. I should just move on.

I was reaching for my bag when the door swung open and The Doctor came through. His cell phone was pressed to his ear. He pointed to the phone, frowning apologetically.

"Yes," he said. "I know." A pause. "I remember." A scowl. I'd never seen him look really annoyed before. I knew that Cecil pushed his buttons sometimes, but he'd always managed to find a cool way of putting the nurse off. This was different.

I slowly eased myself back into the chair.

"Yes," he said. "Yes. We—yes. Okay. We'll talk about it when . . . Right. I'm with a patient now. Of course. I will. I have to go now. Okay, good-bye." He hesitated another moment, then pulled the phone away from his ear, stabbing the screen with his finger to end the call.

"Bad time to talk?" I asked, still poised to leave.

"Quite the opposite." He squared his shoulders and took his seat.

"Sorry. I was afraid that if I kept you much longer you might go."

"Was that—" I asked, then stopped, not sure how to finish the question, or even if I wanted to.

The frown returned. "Wife," he said. That was all.

Silence fell between us. For a moment we sat there, looking around the room rather than at each other. Was it because he'd reminded us of his marriage? That was probably something we should both remember from time to time.

I was curious, but something told me not to pry. Asking questions tends to close people up. That's Psych 101. Better to offer something of yourself and see if you could coax some trust out of the other person.

I took a deep breath. "My husband just got orders for a special assignment. He just found out that he'll be overseas for close to a year."

The Doctor's face cleared as he shifted his focus from his problems to mine. "And you're worried about him."

"I'm worried about me," I said, then wrinkled my nose. "That sounds selfish. I just . . . He's . . . I want him here with me." I wriggled in my seat, uncomfortable. In my head, The Doctor and Marcus belonged to two separate worlds. I'd never talked openly about one with the other.

The Doctor swiveled his chair to examine the photographs taped to his cabinets. "My wife and I used to be like that. We've hit a rough patch," he said. His voice betrayed little, but I saw that the corners of his mouth had turned down. I noted again that he'd taped several pictures of each of his kids, but none of his wife.

"Oh?" It bothered me a little that things weren't right with his marriage. Was he paying so much attention to me just because his wife was distant? Or was this rough patch the result of him paying too much attention to all his female patients?

"We're in counseling," he said, spinning his wedding ring with his thumb. I wondered if he even realized he was doing it. "We got married young, had kids young, I was gone regularly on temporary duty assignments in the beginning . . . now that the kids are getting older and I'm around all the time, we're starting to realize that we don't know each other that well."

"I'm sorry to hear it," I said, not sure if that was true but feeling that it was the right thing to say. "Kids can be like glue, huh?"

"They can distract us from the fact that we've married a stranger."

"Is your wife a stranger?"

He turned back to me. "Isn't everyone?"

"Maybe you can't know anyone else as well as you know yourself, but that doesn't mean people are unpredictable."

He laughed and shook his head. "I bet you were a psych major."

"I just started my master's."

"Ah, well good luck." The sardonic smile gave way to a more genuine one. "It's a lot, isn't it? Kids. Work. Marriage."

"It's a lot, but it's not too much," I protested.

"Hm." He looked down at his wedding band. "Sometimes I wonder."

Looking theatrically from side to side, I shifted to the edge of my seat and leaned in closer. "The worst part about this assignment isn't Marcus leaving."

"What's the worst part?"

I lowered my voice to a stage whisper. "My mother is coming to help with the kids."

The Doctor nodded somberly. "You and your mother aren't close?"

I'd meant to make a joke, but now that he'd taken the punch line seriously, I mulled this over. "I love her. But I have five kids of my own, and I've always been . . . kind of like her mother, too, I guess. She's a free spirit. She lives by her own set of rules."

"So that's why you married into the military," he said, tapping one finger against his lips.

"Now who's psychoanalyzing who?"

"You like rules. You want order. That makes sense."

I folded my arms. "Explain."

He shifted in his chair, getting comfortable, abandoning his usual stiff posture. "Some people gravitate to the military life because they don't like having to think for themselves. Officers might give orders, but there are rules that must be followed. Protocols. You didn't strike me that way, so I wondered, what's the draw for you?"

"But now you've got it," I said, lifting my eyebrows.

"Sure." The Doctor smirked. "Mommy issues."

"Oh, please," I groaned.

"You're good at the game," he conceded. "You walk the walk, talk the talk, et cetera." He waved one hand lazily in the air to illustrate how little he cared about all that. "I know what you're doing. You're playing the game, same as I am. Same as any of us are. You're putting on the show."

"So I'm a fake?" I asked. In my head, the words came out light and sarcastic. In reality, they had a weight to them. No one had ever talked about my life this way, and yet the truth of these words was something I carried with me all the time.

"You're a performer," he said. "You know what's expected of you. Color inside the lines. That doesn't mean you have to paint the sky blue or the grass green."

I opened my mouth in surprise, not sure how to respond. From the corner of my eye, I suddenly caught view of the clock. I checked my watch, but the hands told me the same thing. It was after three.

I jumped up. "I have to go! I'm sorry, I wasn't watching the time." The kids would be out of school before I made it back to my car.

"I'll see you next week," he said, still sitting, still draped across the chair. "You'll keep up with the journal?"

"Of course," I said, collecting my things from the extra chair. "I'll keep adding more protein like we talked about last time."

"I look forward to seeing you again." As soon as the words were out, his smile faded. Maybe he'd remembered that I was someone else's wife, or that my husband was about to be deployed. Maybe he'd just said too much. He rose slowly to his feet, straightened his coat, and shook my hand before I left.

On the way out of the hospital door, it occurred to me that I hadn't brought the article I'd clipped for him from the paper: The Ten Benefits of Eating Chocolate Daily. He'd laugh at that.

I'd have to tell him next week.

● ● ● ●

October came, bringing golden leaves and jack-o-lanterns and lengthy debates over possible Halloween costumes, candied apples and warm cider, sweaters and scarves.

October came, and Marcus left.

Chapter Nine

"I really don't see how you can focus," sniffed Corrina.

"I could focus better if you would stop saying that," I muttered, but I kept my voice so low that I more or less mouthed the words.

Corrina had come to help with the kids while Marcus was deployed. Rather than lightening my workload, which was the idea, I sometimes felt as if I'd gained another child. At that exact moment I had a textbook balanced on my lap while I folded the laundry. Read a sentence, fold a shirt. Read a sentence, match a pair of socks. It gave me time to digest each line, and while the process may not have been efficient per se, it left me feeling as though I were getting somewhere.

"You read, I'll fold the laundry," Corrina said.

I raised my hands in surrender, took my textbook, and scooted over to the far end of the couch. Corrina sat down amid the laundry and began to work. I never failed to be astounded by the number of clothes five kids could dirty in the span of a few days.

I settled down, trying to soak in the chapter in front of me. This section focused on the concept of sublimity. As near as I could make out, the idea was that something could be flawed from a subjective view, but perfect from an objective angle. For example, a pair of shoes might have holes in the toe, scuffed leather on the heel, and a broken eyelet where a lace had pulled through, all things that made it less than perfect. To the owner of the shoes, however, they might feel perfect, having been broken in by their feet over the course of years. Was there another word, I wondered, for something that *looked* perfect but didn't *feel* perfect?

"I can't help but wonder," Corrina began. I closed my eyes and took a deep breath.

"Can't help but wonder what?"

"Oh not now, dear, you're reading. Don't let me interrupt."

"It's fine." I closed my book around my finger to save my place. "See? I'm listening."

"I see how much you take on," said Corrina, balling up a pair of socks and tossing them on the pile. "I told you to do something for yourself, something that feeds your spirit and brings you a sense of peace. Do you ever plan to take that advice?"

"I lost the weight," I told her. "That was for me."

She snorted, waving a jeweled hand dismissively in my direction. "So people think you look better. Do you feel better?"

I bit my tongue.

My mother pushed the clothes aside and gazed at me intently. When she wanted to, she could be almost as intense as The Doctor. "There's an old phrase, honey. Life sucks, and then you die."

"Who said that?" I asked. "Kant? Maybe Marx?"

"Somebody underpaid," said Corrina drily. She knew she was pushing my buttons. She didn't care. "Somebody without a personal life. Someone without a *real* life."

I pointed to the laundry. "This is real life, Mom."

"This is work. Work is the stuff we have to get out of the way before we can live. When you're done with work, you go do more work. What kind of life is that? What makes you happy?"

I was prepared to say something harsh, about how she'd always put her pleasure before her obligations and I wasn't like that. The words stuck in my throat. My family made me happy. Marcus made me happy. Kari and Yasmine made me happy. My classes and my house and the way all the parts of my life fit together, the person I saw when I looked in the mirror and the way I felt inside my skin—all of that made me happy.

And my meetings with The Doctor made me happy.

"See, there." Corrina shook a finger at me and gave a knowing smile. "You've thought of something. I was afraid you wouldn't have an answer."

I shook off the thought. "Feeling responsible makes me happy. Coming through for people."

Corrina folded her arms. "In the dead of night, when your little ones are in bed and your husband is safe beside you and you're drifting off to sleep in your nice house, do you dream about being responsible?"

I bit my lip.

"I didn't think so." Corrina's expression was all smug satisfaction.

"It's selfish," I blurted, thinking of my lengthy meetings in The Doctor's office when I should be cooking or cleaning or getting ahead on my schoolwork.

"Most of the things that we really want are. That's what makes them so meaningful." Corrina rose, turning her back on me and gliding away, mistress of the dramatic exit.

I leaned over to check her abandoned pile of clothes. She'd folded everything haphazardly, leaving sleeves dangling and pant legs askew. I would have to fold it all over again. I opened my book on my lap, shook out a shirt, and set to work.

• • • •

"Have you made any friends in your new program?" Kari asked. She selected a pale green onesie from the display and held it up to Yasmine, who wriggled in the stroller seat.

"Not that one," I said. "She looks like you spilled pea soup on her. And I'm not there to make friends."

Kari traded the offending outfit for one in navy blue. "I just thought you might use the opportunity to get out more, you know? Broaden your horizons and all that. Do something fun with people who like the same things you do."

"We like the same things," I protested.

"You're allowed to have more than one friend, you know." She reached for a hat decorated with pink hearts.

"That's a little much, don't you think?"

She fitted the hat onto Yasmine's head. "I like it. And I'm serious. Get out more. Meet some new people. Try new things. You're spinning your wheels, Ames. Do that too long and you'll burn out."

"Now you sound like Corrina," I protested. "School is new. I'm trying new things. I'm happy where I am."

Kari abandoned the baby clothes for a moment. She looked at me the way Marcus sometimes did when he thought I was fooling myself.

"No," she said. "I'm happy. I know what happy looks like. You want something, Ames. A change."

"I don't know what I want," I admitted

Kari shrugged. "You'll work it out. My advice? Make new friends. Talk to people."

"Now you sound like you're sending me off to kindergarten. *Make new friends. Don't run with scissors.* And you're right, she's cute in that hat."

Kari leaned over to pinch her daughter's cheeks. "She's cute in everything," she said. "And if you don't make new friends by the end of next week, you're grounded, young lady."

"I'll make a note of it," I said.

• • • •

Dark clouds had hung in the sky all day, and just as I made it in the hospital door, the skies opened up. I'd left my umbrella in the car, foolishly confident that the clouds would disperse by the end of my appointment.

The Doctor was waiting in his office when I arrived. He waved me into my chair as if he was greeting an old friend. He'd never said it aloud, but I suspected that he felt the same way with me that I felt with him. Comfortable. Trusting. Like we could put aside our everyday worries and just be . . . free. For a little while, at least. School and family and bills and social obligations waited just beyond the office door, but they never followed me inside.

"You have your journal?" he asked. I handed it over, and he flipped through six months of notes to the current week. He placed one finger on the page, reading item by item, nodding at each line. I could tell when he hit Tuesday, because his smile turned down at the edges.

"Corrina arrived on Tuesday," I said, by way of explanation.

He glanced up at me, lifting an eyebrow. "Corrina?"

"My mother."

The Doctor whistled. "Most people don't call their parents by a first name."

"Most people didn't have Corrina for a mother," I joked.

He handed the journal back. "I suspect that you know where there's room for improvement."

"More lean protein, less comfort food. On it." I tucked my journal back into my bag, and that concluded the business portion of our meeting.

"How's school?" he asked.

I shrugged, pulling a face. "Okay. I don't really feel like I belong there yet."

"You're certainly smart enough," he said.

"But too old."

"Oh, stop." He shook his head. "You'll find your niche. Give the kids a chance. They're not all as dumb as they look."

I couldn't bite back my laughter. "They're fine. Really. They're just so young. They have no . . ." I trailed off.

"No experience," he said, pulling a pen out of his pocket and spinning it between his fingers. He was constantly in motion. "But you do."

I'd been about to say, *responsibilities.* I didn't want to bring that word into the room, though. Corrina had been disgusted with me for putting responsibility before happiness, and in any other place I could have. I wanted to. But at some point, when I hadn't been paying attention, this room was the place I came to get away from that world, the world of dirty socks and bagged lunches and putting on seamless performances.

"Anyway," said The Doctor, "you—"

His words were cut off by a burst of sound, a tinny electronic shriek that echoed down every hallway in the building, grating and out of place. I lurched in my seat, afraid without knowing what to be afraid of yet. The Doctor only rolled his eyes.

"Really? A fire drill? In the rain?"

I covered my ears. "What an awful sound."

The Doctor got up, reaching to pull me out of my seat. "Bring your bag. Who knows how long this will last."

We went out into the hallway, joining a stream of people who all looked about as happy as we were. The crush of people piled up in the hallways, heading for the front doors. Outside, we huddled in a mass along the covered walkways, packed tightly against each other.

"If there really was a fire," I said, "this would be a terrible place for us to stand."

"True," said The Doctor, pointing out into the pounding rain, "but nice weather for it."

"How long do these usually last?"

He shrugged and shook his head, shifting to make room for a large woman who approached the edge of the walkway, gazed out through the downpour toward her car parked somewhere in the enormous lot, and then retreated back into the milling crowd.

"We should go to my car," I suggested suddenly. I don't know why I said it. The idea occurred to me, and before I could question it too closely, the words had come out.

The Doctor looked at me, probably trying to gauge how serious I was being.

"It's dry there," I coaxed.

He looked around at the cold and grumbling people pressed against us. "All right."

"I'll lead the way."

"Ready?" he asked. "Three. Two."

Before he could reach *one*, I took off, shrieking as the rain washed over me but not turning back. The Doctor followed. We passed Cecil, but I only caught a glimpse of his startled expression before I was out among the abandoned cars, headed toward my van, using my key to blink the lights so we would know where to head for safe haven, like sailors watching for a lighthouse along the cliffs of an unfamiliar coast.

• • • •

When I was a girl, my mother took me and my sister to a beach somewhere in the Carolinas. She warned us not to get sand in our eyes and let us go.

Along the tide line, as I played in the surf, my bare feet came down on something soft and sleek. I looked down to see a rippling circle of smooth flesh punctured by two black pinpoint eyes. I gasped, amazed, bending down for a better look. The creature moved away, and I moved with it, riveted by its alien shape, lured by its mystery.

Sting rays, I did not know, have poisonous tails. Their stings are rarely fatal, but the wounds they leave are painful and slow to heal.

That was what things were like with my mother. She warned me against discomfort, but not against danger. I didn't even know the risk I'd taken by following what I should have run from. All I'd seen was beauty, and I'd chased it out to sea.

• • • •

We slammed the van doors behind us just as the rain picked up.

"Good timing," said The Doctor.

I rolled my eyes and pushed my wet hair out of my face. "Not really."

He shook the water out of his hair, then folded his arms and gave an exaggerated shiver.

"If you're cold I can put the heat on," I offered.

He raised his eyebrows. "I like the sound of that."

I stared at him, searching for a comeback that didn't arrive. It was like the moment in Dr. Randall's office, when The Doctor had touched my leg and I hadn't protested. If I scolded him for his forwardness, he'd stop. I said nothing. My silence might not encourage him, but it wouldn't dissuade him, either.

As if he, too, were thinking of that first touch, The Doctor reached across the space between the seats and placed his hand on my knee. We looked at the place where our skin met, as if these were strangers' bodies touching.

I thought abruptly of the general and his strange pass at me. He'd touched my knee in almost the same way during his awkward flirtation. Where The Doctor's fingers rested on my skin, I felt hot. The general's come-on had been absurd because he was no one to me. He'd liked what he saw when he looked at me. His interest was skin deep.

When The Doctor looked my way, he saw into me. He saw who I was.

"What are you thinking?" he asked softly.

"That you aren't the first man to make a pass at me."

"Ah," he said, suddenly hesitant. "This isn't unusual for you?"

"No." I looked across at him. "Not unusual."

"Ah." He pulled his hand away. "Sorry to add to the unwanted attention."

I turned in the seat to look at him. There was that stiff expression, the hard line of his mouth that he hid his feelings behind. I must have been watching him closely to know his expressions so well.

The rain was coming down hard, and the *ping* of drops against the roof of the van was enough to fill the silence for a few long moments. The Doctor stared out the window although there was nothing to see in the downpour. Water obscured our view of the outside world.

"I'll get out the second it lets up," he promised.

"I never said that this was unwanted." I reached for his hand and placed it back on my leg.

He looked at my face, then at the place where we touched, then down at his feet.

"What are you thinking?" I asked.

He turned toward me. "That I—"

I leaned forward, cutting him off. My lips brushed the corner of his mouth. He froze, startled into silence.

That was one expression I'd never seen before.

Up close, I could see the fine lines around his eyes, remnants of sleepless nights. His eyes weren't just blue, they were all blues mixed together. Afternoon shadow already prickled his cheeks, although I was sure he shaved every morning before work.

"Answer the question," I said. My words were so soft they were almost lost in the drumming of the rain. "What are you thinking?"

"That we really shouldn't," he said.

"No," I agreed. "We shouldn't." I let my fingertips drift across his cheek, and he closed his eyes. My heart thrummed. I was bold, maybe too bold, but every passing second made me bolder. I was powerful. It was like watching a movie, but it was also like jumping off a cliff. Unreal, and overwhelmingly real. There was no going back. Only forward.

I kissed him.

When my teeth grazed his bottom lip he let out a little noise of surprise.

Corrina had asked, *What makes you happy?*

All my blood rushed to my head. I felt drunk. People who drink too much like to make excuses for themselves. They say that they didn't know what they were doing, they weren't themselves. I was myself. I was Amy who'd hosted the best parties on campus, I was Amy who'd smuggled a whole case of sparklers into the dorm commons, I was Amy who had once climbed between two fourth-floor balconies on a dare. I'd thought that Amy tamed out of existence, but here she was, teasing The Doctor's tongue with her own, pressing her hand against the back of his neck, pulling him closer.

"I could lose my license," he breathed. The words came out ragged, like he'd had the wind knocked out of him.

"Then go," I murmured as I ran my hand across his chest. "I'm not making you stay. I'm not making you do anything."

"Amy . . . ," he whispered, running his hands through my hair. He did not get out of the car.

I kissed him again. With Marcus—I shouldn't be thinking of Marcus, but how could I not?—I had always been the one who was seduced. He was always the one in charge. I'd been happy to play that role, because that's who I was with him.

When I tugged The Doctor's coat collar, pulling him close for another kiss, I felt him give in to me. That was new. And I liked it.

I slid out of my seat and into his, turning so that I sat in The Doctor's lap. He groaned, sliding one hand up my back beneath my shirt, and the press of his skin against mine was like a live current.

"Have you thought about this?" I asked. "Have you thought about me?" Who talked like that? Maybe I was possessed. Still, I wanted an answer.

He ran his hands from my knees up to my thighs, pushing my skirt higher.

"Amy . . . I don't . . ."

"Don't what?" I asked. "Don't want me?"

He rolled his hips beneath me in answer.

I reached down to pull the seat handle, lowering the back until he lay reclined beneath me, looking up at me with feverish eyes. I leaned in close, making sure to hold his gaze.

"I know what I want," I said. "You."

The Doctor reached down between us, fumbling with the cotton tie on his pants. I pushed his hand away, and the knotted cord came undone beneath my fingers. With one hand, I tugged the hem of his scrubs lower, and he groaned when my fingers closed around him.

"There's still time to leave," I said softly as I leaned down to kiss him. "But we both know that's not what you want."

He growled, pushed my panties aside, and then he was inside me. There was no time for a slow exploration of each other's bodies, but that wasn't what I'd wanted anyway. I wanted the rain pounding down on the roof of the car to isolate us from the outside world, I wanted his hot breath against my throat, his hands on my hips pulling me closer, his tongue tracing the curve of my collarbone. I wanted to hear the changing tempo of my own breath, to feel the moment when the static charge between us became a lightning bolt and I sat upright, gasping, and his back arched against the seat, his hands on my breasts and my name in his mouth and the spread of his warmth between my legs. Afterward, I wanted to lie against him, breathing hard, still amazed at what had just happened between us, not yet afraid of the consequences. I wanted him to run his fingers through my hair, then lift my chin so that we could look each other in the eye. I wanted him to reach down, to press his fingers into the wet warmth between my legs.

"I want you again, right now," he growled.

And it was still raining, and we were still in our own private world, and neither of us was in any rush to leave.

Chapter Ten

I scraped the last of the scrambled egg from my plate and reached for my journal, prepared to make my breakfast entry: *toast, two slices; eggs, two; banana, one medium; coffee, one cup.* It was habit, by then, to record everything I ate. The pen was already in my hand when I paused.

I shouldn't keep the journal. I should cancel all the appointments. I should distance myself from The Doctor in every way. I needed to get him off my mind.

I'd replayed our encounter in the van every night since, remembering the warmth of his hands, the weight of his gaze, the urgency of his kisses.

What if Marcus ever found out?

The moment that The Doctor stepped out of my van, the real world had come rushing back to me. Less than an hour of my life had passed, but that encounter had the power to undo everything I'd worked for. I'd deliberately ignored the possible consequences of my actions, but now they were all I could think about.

Even so, I wasn't sure I regretted what we'd done.

Which was probably the number one reason I should toss the journal and pretend nothing had happened

"Mommy! I can't find my hat!" Lydia called.

"I'm coming." I made a quick note of what I'd eaten, closed the journal, and went to help my island-reared daughter dress for the cold.

• • • •

"High on life?" Corrina asked.

I looked at her across the kitchen island. "What do you mean?"

Corrina leaned on her elbows, giving me a smug mother-knows-best smile. "You seem to be in good spirits."

"Do I?" I asked, putting aside my dish towel. Did I feel happier? I wasn't sure. Thinking about The Doctor made me feel good—until I thought about the potential fallout.

"Oh, don't do that," said Corrina. "Don't get all gloomy just because I've mentioned it. It's very contrary of you."

"It's not that," I said. "I just . . . It's complicated."

"It makes you happy. What's so complicated about that?"

I opened my mouth, but the words stuck in my throat. How could I explain what I'd done, much less to my mother? Of all the people in my life, she'd be the most likely to understand. That didn't really make me feel better.

"No need to explain, I'm just pleased to see you smiling so much." She slid onto one of the stools and folded her hands in front of her. "I wanted to let you know that I'll be heading home tomorrow. You've got everything in hand here. You don't need me."

"It's all right. I've done this before," I assured her.

Corrina cocked her head, fixing me with her gaze. I'd never seen my mother observe me that deeply before.

"I know you think I'm flighty," she said. "I have my own reasons for going home, but do me a favor. Take the compliment. You're a competent woman. You're an excellent mother. You're so . . . in order." She said the word as if it were a foreign concept to her. "We don't live the same way, but I respect what you've made for yourself here. The American dream, isn't it? You've made the life you always wanted for yourself."

I swallowed hard as she gently patted my back. "Thank you," I said. And I meant it.

The trouble was, she was right. I had the life I wanted. Marcus was perfect, an attentive husband and patient father. I loved my marriage. I loved my family.

And I'd risked it. If Marcus found out what had happened between me and The Doctor, how would I explain that I cared about both of them deeply? He'd see it as a breach of trust, and I didn't know if he could ever forgive me. He wouldn't understand that this wasn't about him. I hadn't been driven to search for a lover out of some failing on Marcus's part. I'd gone looking for myself, and I'd found The Doctor.

I wanted what I knew I shouldn't want.

The women of The Coffee would look down their noses at me if word ever got out. It would look bad for Marcus, too, even though I was the one who'd slipped up. What would Kari think? What would my children think?

Marcus's reputation, The Doctor's reputation, The Doctor's rank, and my marriage.

I could lose everything. Both of us could. All of us could.

My mother rubbed my hand. "You turned out pretty well, Amy."

My mother, twice divorced, had ended up alone. She had no everyday companion. No partner. No one who loved her like Marcus loved me. Corrina was content, but I could never live like that. I needed the steady certainty of my husband, the chaos of my family. I wouldn't be happy on my own.

I gripped Corrina's hand tightly. "Thank you, Mom," I said.

• • • •

"Since we've covered our chapters on research theory, I'm prepared to assign a group project."

I looked up from my notes, startled back to reality by the professor's words. I knew that Professor West had planned to give us a large assignment in research theory—it was right there in the syllabus, making up nearly a third of our score in the course—but it hadn't occurred to me that it would be a *group* project.

"I will ask you to break off into groups of four. I'd like you to pick a topic, and over the next four weeks I will ask you to develop a research and mock grant proposal for how you might test that theory." Professor West paused, pushing sharply on his glasses, frowning around at all of us. "I expect you to do your part. Some people, I know, view group projects as an opportunity to slack off and let others do all the work. Rest assured, if you attempt to do so, I will know."

The professor's warnings might frighten some, but the sudden spike in my blood pressure had more to do with the structure of his class than his dire threats. Slackers aside, I had no interest in teaming up with a group of kids half my age to study how porn affects the brain or whether smartphones have a negative impact on our social interactions. What a nightmare.

As I surveyed the classroom with despair, another woman caught my eye. She was close to my age, with a strong jaw and dark eyes. She was looking my way intently, as if willing me to make eye contact. When I did, she gave me a brisk wave, lifting her chin in greeting. I couldn't have said what her ethnicity was: she had black hair that fell to her shoulders in tight curls, warm brown skin, and dark eyes. She lifted one eyebrow slightly when I returned her wave, as if she already knew everything about me and found it slightly amusing.

Maybe she'd singled me out because both of us were older than most of the other students, or because we looked somewhat alike. Either way, her greeting was like a lifesaver thrown my way. I slid out of my chair and headed toward her.

Already the other students were milling around, shaking hands and exchanging high fives. Many of them, it seemed, were already friends. I'd done no socializing since I entered the program. I knew the names of the professors, but my classmates were a mystery to me, and not one that I'd been particularly interested in solving.

When I stood in front of her, the woman leaned forward and rested her elbows on the desk. "Hello," she said. "I'm Sasha, and I'm over the age of twenty-three. Any interest in working together?"

I slid down into the chair beside her. "Sounds like the kind of ice-breaker my kids have to do in school. I'm Amy."

"Except that they're probably given prompts and name tags," said Sasha with a wry smile. "So, Amy, how shall we catch our little group another two members?" Sasha sat up in her chair again, scanning the room.

I looked too, and my eyes caught on a pair of girls in the corner. They were standing close together as if they knew each other, but angled awkwardly as though they weren't comfortable with each other's presence. I sat a little higher and made eye contact with the first girl. She had broad features and long dark hair that fell straight down her shoulders. She elbowed the other girl, whose face was framed by a bright pink headscarf. The second girl turned too, and narrowed her eyes at me. After a moment she nodded and they both made their way toward us.

"Found us some friends, have you?" asked Sasha agreeably.

The first girl approached, bobbing her head. "Hello," she said. "Are you looking for partners?"

The second girl rolled her eyes. "You can be more direct, Nurul."

Nurul nodded. "Yes. Sorry. I am Nurul, and this is Alina. We are looking for partners. Would you like to work with us?"

Sasha raised her eyebrows. "Are you ESL students?"

Alina pursed her lips, as if preparing to defend herself against whatever Sasha might have to say. "Yes."

"This should be fun." Sasha sat back to survey the three of us. "I'll bet you five rounds of your favorite drink that we pick the most interesting topic in this class."

Nurul smiled. "Then we have a group."

From behind his desk, Professor West got up. "Wrap it up, everyone. You'll have opportunities during class to work on your topics, but I suggest exchanging numbers so that you can set up other times to meet and coordinate."

"I can't stand group chats," said Sasha at once. "Phone or email only."

Nurul flipped to a page of her notebook and began to write. "Email is good. We can copy everyone in the chain. I'll keep this page and email everyone tonight." She handed the notebook to Alina, who took it and scribbled down her own information.

"Can we set up a time to meet now?" I asked. "I'll have to find someone to watch the kids if it's on the weekend."

"We could come to your house," Sasha suggested. "If you're comfortable with that. Then you wouldn't need a sitter."

"Oh," I said. "Oh. Well . . ." The idea of two more parts of my world colliding was a little alarming, but I stopped to consider it. "That would be easier," I admitted.

"How about Saturday?" Sasha suggested. "Not too early."

"That could work," I said, still wary of the idea. And after all, why not have them over? I couldn't think of any reason they wouldn't be welcome, and it would make things simpler with the kids. "Let me see how my husband feels about it. Either way, Saturday is good for me."

"I can drive the two of us," said Alina, tipping her chin toward her friend.

Sasha handed me the notebook, and I wrote down my information, including my address. Nurul looked over everything, wrote our names on another page, and tore it out of the pad.

"I'll see you Saturday," she said, and she gave us a brilliant smile.

As we filed out of the classroom, I shook my head to clear it. I hadn't been at all prepared for that exchange, much less to have three near-strangers invite themselves to my house.

The idea was a little exciting, though. When was the last time I'd had anyone new over?

I was almost to my next class before I realized that since the mention of the group project, I hadn't thought about The Doctor once.

• • • •

The kids piled on the couch around me, waving to the screen of my laptop. Marcus waved back from his own screen half a world away. "It's great to see everyone!" he said. "Sorry it's been so long. There was an incident near the last base and we were stuck without power for a few days. How is everyone? Have I missed anything?"

I swallowed as the kids shouted over each other to be heard. *Well, I slept with someone,* I thought. I hoped that my feelings didn't show through on my face.

"I got a B-plus on my math test," bragged Conrad.

Lydia elbowed him. "That's nothing. I got an A in English."

"English is easy," said Conrad, disgusted. "Nobody cares about your A."

"Enough, you two, and please, watch your tone," I said. "Your father will think I've replaced his kids with a bunch of zoo animals."

Marcus laughed. "I'm just happy to see that everyone's fine!" I looked closer and noted the lines around his eyes. He hadn't been sleeping well. Whatever was going on over there was keeping him up at nights.

Eliza lurched suddenly off the couch and disappeared into the next room.

"How's my beautiful wife?" asked Marcus.

"Great," I said. "Smooth sailing."

"How are your classes?"

"We were given a group project in my research methods class. One of the women asked if we could meet here to go over the assignment. What do you think?"

"You're the queen of the castle," said Marcus. "You make the rules."

I nodded thoughtfully. "Okay. If you're comfortable with it."

Before Marcus could say anything else, Eliza shot back into the living room, sliding in her socks across the hardwood floor. "Daddy, look what I drew!"

Marcus squinted at the screen. "Is that the caterpillar from your book?" he asked.

"*The Very Hungry Caterpillar*! Do you like it?" Eliza asked shyly.

"It's wonderful," he said. "Ask Mom to put it on the fridge so that I can see it in person when I get back, okay?"

I wanted to tell Marcus how much I missed him, how much I needed him, how much we all needed him. I was searching for the words when he turned back toward me.

"Hey, Amy, guess who I ran into out here?"

"I'm not even sure where you are," I said. "The desert somewhere . . . Elvis?"

He laughed and shook his head. "Him, too! No, do you remember Rob?"

"Rob," I said blankly, sifting around in my memory. "Rob, Naomi's husband?"

"Ex-husband," Marcus reminded me. "He's remarried now. He was asking about you and the kids."

Guilt had sat low and warm in my belly all through the call, but at the thought of Rob's remarriage I went cold. Naomi had been so lost when she came to see me. I'd tried to reach out to her several times since we moved, but she'd avoided me. Did she have a new family too? Was she happy? I couldn't picture it.

If he ever found out what I had done, Marcus would leave me. I was suddenly sure of it.

Marcus looked away from the screen and nodded to someone I couldn't see. "I should go," he said. "Email me, okay? I want lots of pictures, and I want to see that caterpillar when I get back."

The kids shrieked their good-byes, waving and telling him to be safe. I couldn't get the words out.

Of all the things The Doctor had made me feel, this was one emotion I'd failed to anticipate.

Fear.

• • • •

I set my journal on my nightstand and lay in my bed, looking at it. In less than twelve hours I had an appointment with The Doctor, the first appointment since that day in the van. I remembered the heat of The Doctor's kiss, his hands in my hair, on my thighs . . .

I wanted to go.

I was afraid to go.

This was the bed I shared with my husband. *To have and to hold, until death do us part.* That oath was still true for me. I didn't want to replace Marcus. I didn't want to choose one over the other. When I was with Marcus, I could be truly myself. When I was with The Doctor, I was truly myself. The problem was that there were two parts of me.

What would he think if he went to the office expecting to meet me, and I never showed? I should cancel the appointment. I should at least be direct. He deserved that much from me.

That night I dreamed that Marcus was in the bed beside me, his breathing even, every muscle in his body relaxed. He felt safe when he was here with me, in this bed, in our house, in his life with me.

I woke early, just after dawn, and went downstairs in my pajamas. Stepping out onto the porch, I shivered in the late fall breeze. It was almost winter now.

My hands shook as I turned on my cell phone and called the office. I was shaking from the cold, wasn't I?

It was too early for the receptionist to be in. I left a message, canceling my afternoon appointment.

This is the right choice, I told myself. But for which one of us?

• • • •

"I like your house," Sasha said, folding her jacket over the back of the couch and setting her bag beside her. She'd looked out of place behind a plastic school desk, where the fashionable cut of her dress and her elegant posture stood apart from the jeans and T-shirts that so many of the other students wore. In my house, however, she seemed more at ease, even if she somehow made the room around her look dim by comparison.

She handed me a bottle of wine. "We could open it later, if the girls drink. If not, it's a gift. I appreciate you offering to host. Are your children here?"

"Upstairs," I said, accepting the bottle. "I made them promise to entertain themselves until we're done. Do you have kids?"

Sasha lifted her shoulders and wrinkled her nose in embarrassment. "I've never really wanted them. I guess I'm not very motherly. I make a terrific aunt, though, in small doses."

I perched on the chair across from her, wearing the mask I usually reserved for The Coffee. Something about that thought bothered me, but I couldn't place it.

"So," I said, "have you always lived around here?"

Sasha smiled, tucking her curls behind one ear. "I'm originally from New York. I moved out here for work a few years ago but I got bored. Things got a little claustrophobic there. I thought I should go back to school and start over, but now that I'm surrounded by all these bright young things in their yoga pants and their designer shoes, I'm not so sure." She covered her mouth with a hand to hide her laughter. "Sorry. I don't mean to make fun of them."

"I know what you mean," I said. "I feel like I'm back in high school sometimes. They all look like kids to me."

"Exactly. They're just so idealistic. Sometimes it makes me look down my nose at them because I feel so much more experienced, and sometimes I'm jealous because I feel so much more jaded." Sasha crossed her legs and leaned back, examining me. "You get it, don't you?"

I nodded. "I do."

Sasha sighed. "I hope I don't sound like I think I'm better than everyone."

"No, it's not that," I said. I let myself slump a little in the chair. "I've been living in a bubble for . . . ages, I guess. I'm not used to people just saying what they think."

Sasha cocked her head. "Sounds disingenuous. Who has time for that?"

I felt the grin spreading over my face. "You'd be surprised." I had a sudden mental image of Sasha at The Coffee, turning her knowing expression on everyone.

I felt that same niggling feeling that I'd forgotten something.

The Coffee. The Coffee was today, and I'd completely forgotten. I jumped to my feet, reaching for my phone.

"Can you excuse me for a moment, Sasha? I just remembered that I was supposed to call someone. I'll be right back."

Sasha nodded agreeably, and I darted into the kitchen, fumbling with the screen of my phone. The general's wife and Tanya May and all the rest of them could get by on their own, but I'd completely forgotten that Kari expected me to be there.

Kari answered on the third ring.

"I have to whisper," she said softly. "Yasmine is asleep and since we're leaving in less than an hour . . ."

"I can't go," I told her.

There was a pause. "Oh?"

"I completely forgot about it, and I have classmates over today to work on a group assignment. I'm so sorry." I meant it, too. The Coffee mattered less and less to me these days, but Kari and I had always attended as allies. Missing The Coffee felt like abandoning ship.

"That's okay," said Kari at last. "School comes first. Maybe I'll ditch too."

I wanted to explain to her, to promise that I would make it right, but the doorbell rang at that moment. "Sorry, I have to go."

As I hung up, I felt another twinge of guilt. Poor Kari. I'd have to find a way to fix everything.

Sasha had let Nurul and Alina in, and both young women stood by the door, clinging uncertainly to their coats.

"You have a very nice house," said Nurul shyly, joining Sasha on the couch.

Alina nodded her agreement, and I saw her glancing over at me, reassessing her assumptions.

"So," said Sasha, leaning back and spreading her arms along the back of the sofa. She looked like she was holding court. "Any idea what you ladies would like for a topic?"

Alina shook her head. "I would like it to be something relevant. Not frivolous. Something that matters to people, and that everyone can identify with. I haven't been able to think of anything yet."

Nurul pulled out her notebook. "I made a list. However, I think that many of the topics are repeats of other current studies. I would like us to work on something original."

"I'd like it to be social rather than personal psychology. Something about how people relate to one another," said Sasha. "That's what interests me."

The three of them turned to look at me. I stood with my phone still clenched in my palm, now slick with sweat.

"Secrets," I said.

Nurul's eyes widened, and Alina nodded sharply. "That's a broad subject, but I like the idea."

"Good thinking," said Sasha, tilting her head back to gaze up at the ceiling. Her expression was unreadable from that angle. "Everybody has secrets."

Chapter Eleven

There was something about being around Sasha that made me want to dress more thoughtfully.

I wasn't worried about impressing her. For one thing, Sasha didn't strike me as someone who was easily impressed. For another, I wasn't a sloppy dresser. If I changed my style, it was possible that nobody would notice but me.

Whenever I was around Sasha, though, I felt a little drab. Most mornings I opted for jeans or skirts. I tried to keep my look modern, never giving into the pressed-khaki-slash-Chico's trend that so many mothers I knew gave into. I took pride in my appearance. I looked good, I just didn't necessarily look like *Amy*.

Sasha always stood out, but she always looked comfortable, too. I admired that. I wanted to feel that. I wanted to see someone who was totally me when I caught glimpses of myself reflected in shop windows or on my way past the mirror.

It wasn't a matter of changing my whole wardrobe, I'd decided. I just needed a few bold pieces to work into my usual rotation of outfits, something surprising but flattering.

I was out shopping for just that sort of thing when I first noticed the lump.

I had just wriggled into a scoop-necked white dress with a flared skirt, decorated with a large red-and-black floral print. It fit snugly, and I turned in the mirror, trying to determine if I liked the retro vibe the dress gave off. It seemed a little old-school, but maybe it would work with the right accessories. My gaze traveled critically from the form-fitting bust down toward my hips, and then stopped. The Doctor's diet had paid off in a flatter belly—except for the lump that broke up the otherwise graceful fall of the dress.

I slid my fingers over the slight bulge. It was soft, and although it didn't hurt when I prodded it, it felt wrong. When I pressed harder, it disappeared, only to reappear when I moved my hand away. Strange. I shrugged out of the dress, eyeing the lump in the mirror.

I could see the scar from where The Doctor had made his incision while removing the band. The lump stood out right over the scar. I pressed it again and the scar flattened out once more. When I probed with my fingertips I could feel a tear in the muscle beneath. I lifted my hands away and after a few seconds the lump reappeared.

"Hernia?" I asked my reflection. Whatever it was, it wasn't painful or tender. Still, I should get it checked out.

Which meant making an appointment.

Realistically speaking, I could make an appointment with anyone. I could meet with a physician, not a surgeon, and get some advice, maybe a reference to a new clinic.

On the other hand, The Doctor had been the one to perform the surgery, so he'd know the most about my situation.

You're only telling yourself that as an excuse to see him again, said a little voice in the back of my head.

To prove myself wrong, I compromised, and made no appointment at all.

• • • •

"'Have you thought of a quantifiable way to measure secrets?" asked Alina. "The whole format of our project will depend on how we choose to define our research terms." Her voice was prickly as always, and she looked around at each of us in turn to gauge our responses. Alina's direct manner reminded me a little of Corrina, except that she seemed to care more about other people's opinions than my mother usually did.

Sasha shrugged one shoulder lazily. "It depends on what we want to measure. Are we cataloging the number of secrets people keep, or the impact of secrets on personal relationships, or . . . ?" She let the words trail off, as though encompassing all the other avenues we could pursue.

Our group sat around a cluster of desks, talking quietly so as not to disturb the other teams. At his podium, Professor West was reading a novel and glancing up occasionally to see if he was needed.

"How about types of secrets?" I suggested. "We could come up with some kind of scoring system to see how many participants are keeping secrets about themselves or about other people, that sort of thing."

Sasha shook her head. "I think that's oversimplifying it. What if the secret involves more than one person? We need something that we could reasonably study if we're going to put together a mock grant proposal."

Nurul looked up from the notebook in which she'd been dutifully transcribing the conversation. "What about motivation?" she asked softly. The rest of us turned to look at her. She wavered a little under the intensity of our collective gaze but continued on. "We could do what Amy's suggesting, but focus on people's motivations for keeping secrets rather than the content of the secrets themselves. That should be much easier to quantify."

Without meaning to, I thought of The Doctor. Why hadn't I come clean to Kari, or Corrina, or—it was terrible to even consider— Marcus? My life would turn upside down, of course. Marcus's life would turn upside down. The Doctor could lose his rank, his job, his license, his family.

And I could lose The Doctor.

None of that sounded particularly easy to quantify.

The other women, though, were nodding their heads.

"That's certainly an interesting social question," said Sasha thoughtfully. "It would tell you a lot about a person, why they keep secrets in the first place. Good thinking."

Nurul blossomed under this praise.

"Would we set predetermined questions?" asked Alina. "Or ask people for general descriptions of their story and break down their responses after the fact?" Although her speech was still crisp, it lacked the bite of defensiveness that her voice so often held. Like Sasha, she was taken with the idea.

The conversation was hitting a little close to home. But it interested me too. What kind of secrets did Sasha have? Or, now that I thought about it, Kari? What kinds of things did people hide from each other?

It seemed to me, suddenly, that there was a real world completely hidden from me. From all of us. We looked at each other and filled in what we didn't know with our own assumptions. We were captivated by the shiny, level surface of things and rarely bothered to look closer and witness the hidden landscape beneath.

• • • •

I hadn't seen Kari since I'd missed The Coffee. We were closing in on Christmas, which on one hand meant an end to the semester, and on the other meant an endless series of holiday parties and shopping trips that had to be balanced with final projects and exams.

I called Kari three weeks before the end of the semester. She picked up on the second ring.

"Hi!" she exclaimed. "What are you doing right now?"

"Sitting on this couch and missing your lovely face," I said. "Why?"

"Raife just put Yasmine down for a nap. Do you have any idea how long it's been since I left the house on my own? Invite me over. Please. Get me out."

I laughed, happy to hear her sounding so much like her old self. "I'm childless until sometime after four," I told her. "Come anytime."

A quarter of an hour later, Kari barreled through my door without knocking.

"This is amazing," she said. "No baby. No husband. I could sing as loud as I wanted in the car on the way over without worrying I'd make anyone cry."

"You could have a drink," I suggested. "One of my classmates brought some wine over during a study group."

Kari shook her head. "Thanks, but I'm still breastfeeding."

"Right. Sorry." I sighed. "I'm not trying to corrupt you, I swear."

"I could do with some corruption. I've been spending too much time with Tanya May."

I smirked. "Does Tanya May know how you spent spring break of senior year?"

"Oh my God." Kari howled with laughter. "She'd spend less time asking if I'll send Yasmine to vacation Bible school when she's old enough, and more time sprinkling me with holy water. Not even Raife knows about that particular road trip."

As Kari hooted over the old memory, I felt the urge to tell her all about The Doctor. Despite the fact that we'd lived so far apart for so long, I knew almost everything about her. She knew almost everything about me.

Almost.

"Kari," I said, and my serious tone stopped her laughter short.

"Hey, Ames. Is something wrong?"

I took a deep breath. I should tell her. I should ask her what to do. The whole story could come tumbling out of my mouth in one long breath, and she would know, and she would understand. I knew she could keep a secret.

And then I thought of the conversation with my classmates, and what The Doctor stood to lose if our secret got out. It wasn't only my story or my risk to take.

I swallowed my confession and lifted the hem of my shirt instead. Kari leaned forward, confused.

"What is that?" she asked, pointing to the lump.

"I think it's a hernia," I said.

Kari looked up at me in alarm. "Have you had it checked out?"

"Not yet."

"Ames!" exclaimed Kari, clearly disapproving.

I held up my hands to surrender, letting my shirt fall in the process. "I just want to make sure I can schedule a surgery," I said in my most soothing voice. "With Marcus abroad and Corrina back at home . . ."

"Oh!" said Kari. "You need someone to watch the kids. Of course I will."

I blinked at her. "That's, I mean, that's really nice of you, but that's not why I called."

Kari elbowed me, careful to avoid my stomach. "Come on, you'd do the same for me if Raife were deployed. We'll figure something out. It's doable."

I elbowed her back. "You're the best, Kari. You really are."

"So you keep telling me," said Kari, feigning a yawn. "I hope you appreciate how marvelous I truly am."

"Every day," I said.

"Would you like to know what you missed at the last Coffee?" she asked, her grin mischievous.

"My gratitude only extends so far. It's bad enough to hear it all in person without having to go through a play-by-play. Tell me about *you*," I said.

She launched into a lengthy story about their plans for the holidays, whether they would go to Raife's parents' place or hers, and the ongoing debate about when they should start planning for a second child. We talked until we heard the front door open.

"Mom?" called Conrad.

Kari jumped to her feet. "Did you say four? Geeze. I gotta run."

"Stay for dinner," I offered.

She hesitated. "I'd love to. I just feel bad leaving Raife. You get it, right?"

"Of course I do," I said, following her to the door. "I know how it is."

"See you soon," said Kari, pulling on her shoes. "Bye, Conrad!"

We waved as she drove off, and I went back inside to hunt up some after-school snacks.

• • • •

After Kari left, I found myself sitting on the couch, turning my phone over and over in my hands. Kari was right. I should go in, and soon—if I needed a surgery to fix the hernia, the ideal time to do it would be over the break so that I could recover before classes started again. Anyway, the longer I put it off, the more likely it was to become a serious health issue. That's what I'd done with the lap band, and I'd promised never to let things get so bad again.

I could think of a hundred reasons to get this checked as soon as possible, and only one reason not to.

I wasn't sure I was ready to see him again.

I thought about The Doctor every day. No matter what I tried to tell myself, I missed him. I'd faithfully kept up with my food diary, the promise of another appointment always tempting me, and my rational mind always aware that going back would be asking for trouble. Now, though, I had to. It was the only responsible choice.

Thus convinced, I opened my phone and found the hospital's number in my contacts. I punched *call* before I could stop myself and held my breath until the receptionist picked up.

• • • •

I made my appointment for the next day, right after classes. I was glad that it wasn't a day that the research class met. There was no way I could have focused enough to pull that off.

As I drove to my appointment, I couldn't help looking over at the passenger seat. I kept imagining his face, the way he'd moved beneath me, the tempo of his breath, the feel of him . . .

I focused on the road.

At the hospital, I parked in an unfamiliar section of the hospital's lot. I didn't want to think about my last meeting with The Doctor any more than I had to. This time, I was going to behave.

Cecil met me at the desk, his eyebrows lifted in exaggerated surprise.

"Why, Amy, looking fabulous as always," he said. "I haven't seen you in a while."

If I hadn't been so on edge, I might have had a witty retort. Instead, all I managed was, "Yes, but I'm here now."

"So you are," he said, and turned to lead me back to the exam room. I followed mutely, while a tiny voice in the back of my head whispered, *He knows.*

Cecil took my height and weight in the hallway before we went through. As he balanced the scale he flashed me a smile. "Looking great," he said.

I wasn't sure how to read Cecil. There was something in his manner that told me he didn't care if people liked him so long as they took him seriously. I wasn't sure I did either.

In the exam room, I settled into the chair while Cecil made small talk. He remembered Marcus's name and how many kids I had even though he couldn't keep their ages straight. I answered him mechanically, my eyes constantly flicking to the door.

Cecil didn't bother asking questions about my hernia. He must have known that I wouldn't answer until The Doctor came in.

At last the door swung open, and every muscle in my body tensed. *I will be good, I will be good, I will be good*, I promised.

The man on the other side was blond, maybe in his late twenties, and I had never seen him before in my life.

He held out a hand to me. "You must be Amy. Pleased to meet you. I'm Captain Jones."

"Nice to meet you too," I said. I snuck a furtive glance at Cecil. He was watching my expression closely.

CPT. Jones was in uniform. It looked like he would be attending to me today. Had The Doctor switched appointments to avoid me? Was he mad at me for disappearing, or had he used me and now wished I had the good sense to stay away?

It doesn't matter, I thought. *This will make things easier.*

CPT. Jones straightened the jacket of his uniform. "Could you tell me more about what's going on? The notes say you're in for a hernia." He sat down in The Doctor's chair.

"I noticed it a few days ago in a department store, while I was trying on clothes," I said, aware that my words sounded clipped and overly formal.

CPT. Jones nodded sympathetically. "Could I see the site?" he asked, pulling on a pair of blue gloves. "If you'd like to change into a gown, we can step out for a moment."

"No, I'd rather not," I said, moving to the exam table and lifting up the hem of my shirt. I'd avoided wearing a dress for exactly this reason. I hadn't wanted to lie back in front of The Doctor in a loose paper gown. I didn't much fancy doing the same around CPT. Jones, either, never mind Cecil.

CPT. Jones was palpating the hernia when the door swung open again. I nearly choked.

It was The Doctor.

I swallowed. My mouth was suddenly dry, and I could hear my heartbeat pounding in my ears. I realized that I was holding my breath. I'd remembered what he looked like, but I'd forgotten the sheer physicality of him, the way the whole room seemed to reorient toward him the moment he walked in. His presence pulled at me like a magnet, and I wanted nothing more than the feel of his hands on me.

I'd almost forgotten CPT. Jones was there until he spoke.

"Looks like an incisional hernia," he told The Doctor.

The Doctor took a few steps toward me and looked at where CPT. Jones's fingers still rested, reached out a hand, then shook his head slightly and folded his hands behind his back.

"Agreed," he said. "Not surprising. That's relatively common under these circumstances." He looked up to meet my gaze, his blue eyes widening slightly as they had right before I first kissed him, and I felt a flush creeping up my neck.

"Are you sure?" I asked innocently. "Maybe you should take a look."

Cecil frowned.

"Of course," said The Doctor. He reached out to touch the old scar. When his fingers brushed across my skin, I had to bite back a sigh. His touch resonated across my body like ripples on the surface of a pond.

"Yes," he said. "That's definitely what it feels like. And you said it doesn't bother you?"

"It's not painful."

"I didn't mean pain, necessarily. For example, are you more aware of it when it's raining? Changes in pressure can affect this sort of thing."

I remembered water pouring down the windshield, the drum of raindrops off the roof of the van.

I swallowed. "Rain doesn't make a difference. It feels the same all the time."

He was so bold. Didn't he see how Cecil watched us? Or maybe he noticed but didn't care. His arrogance was thrilling. How could such a small touch set me on fire like that?

When he pulled his hand away I still felt the ghost of his caress.

CPT. Jones chattered on, but I wasn't listening. My ears had stopped working. I couldn't focus on anything but The Doctor. *I will be good, I will be good*, I told myself.

But that had been a lot easier before The Doctor showed up. I hadn't known then how badly I wanted him.

"Thank you, CPT. Jones," said The Doctor. He waved me back to the chair, and I went. "I think we can all agree on the diagnosis, Amy, given your surgical history. We'll make a pre-op appointment at your convenience. I know you have a history of putting off treatment as long as possible."

"I'm trying to do what's best for my health," I said, lifting my eyebrows significantly. *I'm trying to do the right thing.*

"Following through on medical treatment is an important part of any wellness program," said The Doctor. "You are your own best advocate in terms of making sure that you get the care you need." *Tell me what you want.*

I swallowed. "I'll schedule something right away."

"This surgery will be like a fire drill. In and out." A smile played across his lips.

As if I could forget the last fire drill.

Sensing that I was flustered, CPT. Jones cocked his head. "If you're anxious about this procedure, there's no reason to be. The care here is excellent, and this is a simple procedure."

"That's always been my experience." I smiled as casually as I could manage. "I know I'm in the best possible hands."

I could feel The Doctor's focus on me as I spoke to CPT. Jones, but I kept my face turned toward the younger man and gave him a pleasant smile.

His part in the appointment done, CPT. Jones bid me a warm good-bye and left. Cecil hovered over us for a moment before taking the hint and following the captain out.

And then we were alone.

If I walked out of the room right now, what had happened between us before could be dismissed as a freak occurrence, a moment of impulse, an anomaly. Why was it so hard for my body to follow my head's advice?

"Well," said The Doctor. "I wondered if I'd see you again." He was spinning his wedding band on his finger, something I'd seen him do before when he was distracted. "I thought you'd disappeared. It was . . . startling, to see your name on the schedule today."

I searched for a witty response, but being left alone in the room had turned me inside out. Instead of the coy remark I'd hoped for, what I said was, "I missed you."

The Doctor smiled. "You're making this very hard for me."

The Doctor rose from his chair, crossing the space between us. I stood at the same time.

I'll behave, I'd promised myself. *I'll be good.* But I wasn't sure those were promises I could keep.

The Doctor reached up, cradling my face in his hands. He looked like a man who'd lost a war he hadn't wanted to fight in the first place.

He kissed me.

One corner of my mind was aware of the door and the hallway beyond, the people moving past who might step in at any moment, who might hear anything. They would know who I was, and who The Doctor was.

He pressed against me, and I fell back a step, then another, until my hips bumped against the edge of the exam table. I put out one hand to stop myself from stumbling and winced at the crinkle of the white paper beneath.

"I keep thinking about you," The Doctor whispered. "I couldn't stop."

"Please don't stop," I whispered back.

He kissed me again and pushed me against the table in reply. His hands roamed over my back, pulling at me so that we were pressed together.

I'd worn jeans rather than a skirt, an extra precaution against any misbehavior. When The Doctor pulled away for a moment, I fumbled with the buttons, cursing my foresight. Every moment we spent in that room was another chance for someone to walk in, but there was no way I was going to change my mind now. I wanted him fiercely.

"I imagined what it would be like if we could take our time." He breathed a laugh. "Turns out, I don't have the self-control."

"I need to feel you *now*," I murmured.

There was no time to remove much clothing, no time for teasing or seduction. There were only our hands and our mouths, the gasping, grasping moments of pleasure, his breath hot against my neck and my teeth pressed into the soft flesh inside my cheeks to keep myself from crying out as he entered me.

Chapter Twelve

I didn't schedule the surgery right away.

For one thing, there were the holidays. I had three children who still believed in Santa Claus and two who were on the fence, a family get-together that required a lengthy car trip, and a Christmas bazaar that I'd volunteered to staff. The kids and I were putting together a big care package to send Marcus and his soldiers for the holidays, and I needed to get that topped off and sent well ahead of time.

There was also schoolwork. On top of the exams, I'd agreed to co-write our draft of the grant proposal with Sasha, while Nurul and Alina tackled the research guidelines.

It was strange to sit in the living room with my children, all of us doing our schoolwork at once, but as the end of my first semester approached, I found that I was starting to enjoy family homework hour.

Besides, before the surgery, I'd need a pre-op appointment. I wasn't sure if I was putting off my next meeting with The Doctor or savoring the anticipation of seeing him again.

• • • •

"This is good," said Alina, taking one last look over the grant write-up. We'd shared drafts of it between the four of us and polished it to perfection. "We could probably submit this for consideration by the university."

"Maybe we should," said Sasha, tapping one heel thoughtfully against the floor. Then she shook her head. "But who has the time?" Nurul frowned down at the stack of our final papers.

"I will miss working with you," she said. "To be honest, I was not looking forward to being in a group, but I think we have done very well together."

Sasha laughed and winked at me. "I know exactly what you mean. It's been a pleasure."

Alina suddenly leaned forward. I was used to her being a bit bossy and prickly, but now a shy smile tugged at her lips.

"All this talk of secrets," she said. "Can we play a game? Let's each tell each other a secret."

"I like it. What do you think, Amy?" asked Sasha. "Shall we play?"

"Sounds a bit silly to me." I swallowed my misgivings. "But why not?"

"I'll go first, then," said Sasha. She leaned in conspiratorially, lowering her voice to a whisper. "I was once proposed to by a man who asked me to move home with him to India and become his first wife."

"*First* wife?" I repeated.

"Didn't you like the idea of sharing?" asked Alina mischievously.

"Sharing wasn't the problem," said Sasha breezily. "I just don't see myself as the marrying type. Who's next?"

"I have a girlfriend," said Alina, hiding her smile behind her hand. "Keisha. We're moving in together. My parents don't know yet."

Sasha whistled.

Nurul cleared her throat. "I do not want to start my own practice."

"That's not a secret," scolded Alina.

"It is a secret from my grandfather," said Nurul. "This is what he wants me to do. It is why he is helping me pay for school. I would rather teach."

Sasha patted her hand. "You'll figure something out."

Nurul nodded gratefully.

Then the three of them turned to look at me.

For a moment I actually considered blurting something about The Doctor. What would they care? It wasn't as if they knew anyone else I knew. It was entirely possible that I'd never see any of them once this class was over.

But the moments I'd stolen with The Doctor were all mine. I was too greedy to share them.

"My mother brought home an expensive bottle of whiskey from Ireland one year. She had this ritual of only drinking one shot on her birthday. My sister and I got our hands on it when we were in college. There was barely anything left by the time we realized how much we'd downed."

"And?" asked Nurul.

I grinned. "We refilled it from a twelve-dollar bottle of Jack Daniels. Every year she takes a shot of Jack and insists it's Ireland's finest."

The four of us parted ways laughing, handing in our papers on the way out. I was halfway down the hallway when Sasha called my name.

I turned back to her. "Yes?"

"Do you want to go out for a drink sometime? It won't be as clandestine as a sip from your mother's liquor cabinet, but I have some friends you might like." I had never seen Sasha hanging out with any of our classmates. I wondered what her friends would be like.

"Oh." I drifted back her way, not sure what to say. My mental calendar was full of art classes, swim meets, and all the other after-school activities that the kids had signed up for, never mind my own commitments.

Sasha noticed my hesitation. "If you don't want to—"

"It's not that," I assured her. "Just, with the kids, it's difficult."

"So find a babysitter," said Sasha.

"Yeah," I said, warming to the idea. "Yeah, okay."

"Great. I'll call sometime." She waved and headed off in the opposite direction.

• • • •

I scheduled my pre-op during the holiday break, before classes started again in January. That way I could time the surgery for spring break so I'd have time off to recover without losing ground in my classes.

Marcus Skyped in for a long call on Christmas Eve. The kids opened their presents while he watched, exclaiming and showing off their new toys.

"Pencils, Daddy!" exclaimed Lydia, brandishing the new set of colored pencils she'd received. Conrad pored through a collection of *Calvin & Hobbes* that his grandmother had picked out for him, and Margie bounced around the room on an inflatable rubber pony, while the twins puzzled out how to use their new rubber band loom to finish a pair of bracelets.

"That's quite the pony," said Marcus. "Does it have a name?"

Margie looked down in surprise. "I don't know. Flowers?"

"Flowers is an excellent name for a pony," said Marcus seriously, but I could see that he was amused.

Could I have chosen a better man to have kids with? I thought, watching him watch them. *I can't imagine one.* I wished he could have been there beside me, holding me close with one arm while the twins decorated themselves with colorful bracelets. I'd hoped that it would be easier during this deployment since the kids were older, but I missed him as much as I ever had.

"I'm going to step out for a moment," I told the kids. "I need to talk to Daddy about something."

The kids didn't take much notice as I carried the laptop to the kitchen.

"Amy? What's wrong?" asked Marcus.

I could have asked the same of him. He looked tired, but I knew that he couldn't explain what was happening to them over there. The best I could do was keep from adding to his worries.

"I thought you should know that I'm having a minor surgery soon. Nothing dangerous," I rushed to assure him. "It's just a hernia. No big deal."

"You're sure?" he asked. "I hate the idea of you having to go through another surgery, especially while I'm away . . ."

"Oh, Marcus." I wanted him with me right then, to be able to hold him, to be held by him. "Don't worry. I promise, I'll be fine. Kari's going to cover the kids, and I'll have a few days before I have to go back to school. Don't worry about it. You've got enough to deal with."

Marcus ran one hand over his head. "I just wish I could be there for you."

"You are here for me. I know that."

"You know what I mean."

"I do. And I appreciate it." I sighed. "And I miss you. And I love you."

"I really can't tell you how much I love you too," he said.

I carried the computer back into the other room, and the kids took turns saying good night and Merry Christmas to their father. It was absurd to think that a man in a war zone was worried about me over a minor surgery, but I understood where he was coming from. The farther away you are from something you care about, the more you realize how hard it would be to live without it.

• • • •

Cecil didn't sit in on the pre-op. It was just me and The Doctor, like it had been for our nutrition follow-ups. Things had changed a little since then. The air between us was electric.

"Do you have any questions about this surgery?" The Doctor asked. His eyes kept traveling up and down the length of my body. His attention made me warm all over, but at least this time I had the restraint to keep my hands to myself. I needed to stay in control if we were going to get through this hernia repair.

"Not really. It sounded pretty standard. Same prep and everything, right? I know the routine."

"Correct. You shouldn't need a long recovery period, either. We'll be doing this laparoscopically using a synthetic mesh. We won't be making any new incisions into the muscle tissue."

"Good." I patted my belly. "Five kids have done enough damage."

He stopped eyeing me up and met my gaze, abruptly somber. "Are you unhappy with how you look? I was under the impression that since your nutrition program you were comfortable in your body."

When he was looking at my legs, my shoulders, my breasts, I felt confident and attractive. Now that his attention had shifted to my inner life, I squirmed under his gaze.

"I'm not unhappy." I fumbled for words, but there was no reason not to be frank with him. We had nothing to hide from each other. "I do sometimes wish that my stomach was a little flatter. I've lost all the extra weight, plus some. I've tried sit-up routines, but even with the diet it's still . . ." I put my hand self-consciously over my stomach. "Pouchy."

"Have you considered plastic surgery?"

I pursed my lips. "Are you suggesting that I need it?"

His low laugh sent tingles racing down my spine. "I think we both know how I feel about your body. It's your happiness that's a little more of a mystery to me."

I tapped my fingers on the arm of my chair. "Okay. Yes, maybe I've thought about it."

"I could recommend someone to you," he said, reaching into one of his drawers for a card.

I shook my head. "Thanks, but no thanks. I don't really want someone else doing it."

He paused in his search through a stack of business cards and pamphlets. "You mean you want me to do it?"

"I trust you," I said. "So, yes, I would prefer you."

"Abdominoplasty isn't really my area of expertise," The Doctor said. "I'm not licensed to do plastic surgery."

"Okay." I folded my hands and looked down at them. "I understand."

He was silent for a long time. When I looked up, he was spinning his wedding ring over and over on his finger.

"I'll already be in there," he said. "It might require a little more recovery time for you, and I'll have to be careful about who's assisting on the surgery. Labeling shouldn't be too much of a problem."

"I can't ask you to do that for me. I would feel horrible if you got in trouble." It occurred to me that this conversation might be the riskiest thing we'd done in a hospital room, which was saying something.

"If that's what you want, I'll make it happen." He stood up and brushed his hands, closing the conversation off.

I was about to say more, but there was a knock on the door, and a second later Cecil poked his head in.

"You're needed in the ER."

"We're done here," said The Doctor. "I'm on my way. Make an appointment on your way out, Amy, and I'll see you then." He'd always taken such good care of me, helping me manage my health. Now he was about to take this risk for my happiness.

"Thank you," I said, although that barely scratched the surface of my gratitude.

We shook hands, letting the contact linger, but that was all.

• • • •

Three days before the surgery, Kari came over to see what she'd gotten herself into.

"Raife's going to swing by at some point to help out," she said. "I'm just figuring out how to keep track of one kid's needs, never mind six."

"They'll be good," I promised, giving my children the evil eye. They all nodded in agreement, except for Conrad, who was too busy playing something on the tablet to worry about things like social graces.

"I'll go shopping the day before the surgery," I said, leading Kari to the kitchen. "The kids have school through Wednesday, so they'll be out of your hair most of the day until then."

Kari bounced Yasmine on her hip. "It's okay, Ames. I know I talk about being out of my depth, but I'll survive, I promise."

"I really appreciate this," I said for what felt like the millionth time. "If there's anything I can do to pay you back, let me know."

A secret smile crept onto Kari's face. "You could keep an eye on Yasmine for me in August. Just for a couple of days."

"Why?" I asked. "What's happening in August?"

Kari's smile widened, and she rubbed her belly.

"What? No! Didn't you two just start trying? I'm so happy for you!" I patted her belly, then pulled her into a bear hug.

"I know, it didn't take much practicing this time," said Kari with a smirk, adjusting her daughter onto her other hip.

"You tell me when, and I'm there," I promised.

"I will," said Kari. "Don't tell anyone else yet, okay? It's still early days."

I crossed my heart, locked my lips, and threw away the key.

● ● ● ●

"Okay," said the nurse, "you're here for the hernia repair and the . . . what the heck is this?"

"Sorry?" I asked.

She frowned at her screen. "It looks like there's another procedure listed, but I've never seen it before, and I definitely can't pronounce it."

I adjusted my bag on my shoulder, trying to keep my expression neutral. "I think they're doing some kind of related work while they have me under."

The nurse pulled a face. "Interesting. Well, okay, you can come on back."

I'd driven myself this time. I wished that Marcus *could* have come, if only to see me off and wish me luck, but it would be months before he came home. The semester would be practically over.

As she led me back through the halls, the nurse looked over her shoulder at me. "Complications from another surgery, huh? That's too bad. Don't worry, honey, we'll get you all sorted out."

I met The Doctor's gaze through the window just before the nurse opened the door. He nodded to me, and although his face was covered with a mask, I could tell from his eyes that he was smiling. Something told me it would take more than minor surgery to get my life back to what it had been.

All I said, though, was, "Yes, thank you. I know you're right."

Chapter Thirteen

Just as The Doctor had promised, I recovered from my surgery much faster the second time around. The site was still tender when I touched it and had taken on a mottled purple tinge, but it didn't hurt. I felt fine, and although I was moving a little more slowly, that seemed like usual post-surgery sluggishness.

I was scheduled for a post-op a week after the surgery, and The Doctor had called a few times to check on me. I appreciated the care in his voice when we spoke. He seemed to agree with my assessment that I was recovering nicely. I was confident he'd give me the all-clear in the exam.

The Doctor, however, examined the bruising closely. "This doesn't look like it's draining correctly."

"Draining?" I pulled a face. "And what does that mean?"

"You're bleeding a little bit where we made the incision. That's normal." He pulled away at last. I missed the contact, but it was hard to enjoy his touch when we were talking about surgical side effects.

"So what's the problem?"

"During the surgery, I placed a drain that would allow excess fluids to escape. It seems to have slipped out of place. What I'm seeing here is a subdural hematoma. The blood vessel is leaking a little bit, and since it isn't draining, it's just building up under the skin. The vessel will eventually repair itself, but in the meantime it needs to be aspirated."

"This sounds like it will involve needles," I said, none too thrilled.

He laughed. "It does indeed involve needles." He rubbed my arm comfortingly, then smoothed my hair, caressing my cheek as he did so. "Don't worry, you know I would never hurt you."

I adjusted my body on the table, covered my face with my hands, and took a deep breath. "Okay, then let's get on with it."

The needle in question was the biggest I'd ever seen. I watched in horror as The Doctor fixed it to the syringe.

"This is the part where you close your eyes, Amy," The Doctor teased. I followed his instructions and tried not to squirm as he sunk it into the purple bruise. "I'll be gentle."

To anyone peering in the door, we would have made a purely medical tableau. The Doctor bent over my side, blue-gloved fingers holding my flesh taught, the bright needle drawing out my blood. Physical contact without any direct touch. A purely sterile interaction.

I couldn't stop thinking about how much I appreciated his care, how happy I was that we'd crossed paths. My thoughts strayed toward our last meeting alone in this office. The press of his hip bone. The crinkle of the exam table paper. The stifled, shuddering breaths.

"Are you all right?" asked The Doctor. He must have noticed the change in my breathing or the sudden tension in my limbs.

"Fine," I said, looking toward the ceiling. "I'm fine."

By the time he finished, the bruising had shrunk by half and the scar site was no longer soft and puffy to the touch.

"So is it fixed?" I asked.

He twisted the needle off the syringe and shook everything into a medical waste bag. "For the moment. I wouldn't be surprised if it needs to be aspirated again before it heals."

"So I'll make another appointment," I said.

"I think that would be wise," he said as he cleaned my side and applied a small dressing.

I reached down to grab his hand as he pulled away. "Thank you so much."

"People don't usually thank me for poking them with needles," he observed.

"Oh, stop it." I couldn't stop my smile. "I mean, no one has ever put themselves on the line for my happiness before. Not like this." I squeezed his hand. "There is no way I could ever repay you."

The Doctor raised his eyebrows and gave me a suggestive smile.

I let go of his hand and pushed it away playfully. "I'm serious. Thank you."

The Doctor gave my shoulder a soft squeeze to let me know he appreciated what I'd said. "How are you feeling besides this?" he asked.

We moved easily around each other, but I was still distracted by the motion of his fingers, the shape of his lips, the deep blue of his eyes. He was watching me the same way—his gaze occasionally drifting across my body and then returning suddenly to meet my own.

"I'm ready for the winter to be over," I said. "I'd forgotten how crazy you go when you're stuck in the house all the time."

"Cabin fever." He nodded. "That's one of the reasons I go hiking whenever I can. There are some good trails around the city."

"I haven't had much chance to explore."

"I like to take my dogs out to the park. You pass it on the way here. It's bigger than it looks, and it's got miles of little back trails. If you stay off the main thoroughfares you can pretty much avoid running into people."

"Do you go there a lot?"

"Every Sunday morning, rain or shine. If you ever need someone to show you the trails, let me know."

I was used to thinking of The Doctor in the context of his job. I hadn't spent a lot of time wondering what he did on his own, or how he spent his free time. Now that he said it, though, it was easy to imagine him under the trees with nobody but his dogs for company, avoiding human contact to give himself time to think. The picture made me smile.

"How's school?" he asked.

Our conversation drifted, as it always did, and by the time I looked at the clock again, an hour had passed. Why was it so easy to lose track of time with him? Why did his gaze reassure me that I was safe with him?

Why did I care so much about him?

The clock would have to wait today. I was in no rush to leave.

• • • •

I was just clearing the dishes from dinner when the phone rang.

"Hello, Amy," said Sasha's voice on the other line. "Any interest in getting that drink? I could use a night out."

I opened my mouth to tell her that I couldn't—but why not? The kids were already fed and bathed. Cleaning up could wait until the morning. My side had felt fine since my appointment the day before. "If the sitter can make it on short notice, I'm in," I told her. "Let me call you right back."

One of the neighbor's kids sometimes sat for me. She was home when I called, and when I promised a tip on account of the timing, she agreed at once.

I called Sasha back immediately. "Okay, I'm free. What's the plan?"

"Can you be out in an hour?"

I did a quick mental calculation. "Sure, okay."

"There's a place out your way you might like. Callahan's. Ever been?"

"I've heard good things, but I haven't had a chance to go."

"You'll love it. I promise."

The moment we hung up, I rushed to my bedroom to change into something worthy of a girls' night out. Jeans and a T-shirt weren't going to cut it.

I'd narrowed it down to three dresses when the doorbell rang. I settled on the floral-patterned dress I'd bought the day I discovered my hernia and rushed to answer.

By the time the babysitter had reviewed the kids' ground rules and the Friday-night traffic had been braved, I was fifteen minutes late for my night out with Sasha.

"Sorry to keep you waiting," I said, trying to cover my breathlessness with the removal of my coat and gloves.

"No worries," said Sasha breezily. "I just got here." The half-empty glass with its melted ice cubes told another story.

Callahan's was an upscale establishment. The lights were dim but not enough to make the room gloomy, and when I glanced over the drinks menu, each option featured a lengthy description of the various ingredients and the drink's history.

Before I could say anything more to Sasha, the bartender appeared.

"What can I get you to start?"

"Oh, I'll have . . ." I let my finger skim down to the first drink I recognized. "A mai tai."

"Modern, 1940, or hibiscus?" he asked.

I looked at the menu, looked at Sasha, and shrugged. "Hibiscus?"

"Good choice," said Sasha. "We'll also have two shots of whiskey, on my tab. Something Irish."

"Oh, I—"

"Don't worry, I don't usually push shots," she said, waving the bartender off. "This one's in honor of you and your sister."

I laughed. "Do we need something in honor of your proposed engagement? Bombay Sapphire, maybe?" I wiggled my eyebrows.

"Gin isn't my drink of choice," said Sasha with mock solemnity.

The bartender returned and set the drinks in front of us. Sasha and I raised our glasses in a little toast.

"To secrets," said Sasha.

"To secrets," I repeated.

We lifted the glasses and tipped the fiery liquid down our throats. I was braced for the burn of a bottom-shelf whiskey that would leave me cringing, but whatever this was had a smooth finish and tasted slightly of smoke.

"I'm glad you were able to come out tonight," said Sasha.

"Me too. Thank God for babysitters."

"To the sitter," said Sasha, lifting her drink. We clinked our glasses in a toast.

"So," Sasha continued, "you were a stay-at-home mom, but now you're back in school, living for yourself again." She took another sip of her drink, leaving me to elaborate if I wanted to.

"I was living for myself when I was a full-time mother," I said. "I'm just ready for a change."

"That part I get," said Sasha. She looked at me out of the corner of her eye. "So, Amy. That cute little secret of yours. Please tell me it was a cover-up to spare the impressionable young women in our group."

It was my turn to buy some silence with a sip of my hibiscus mai tai. It was good, and I let it sit on my tongue for a moment before swallowing.

"Don't tell me I'm the only one who copped out on that question."

Sasha grinned. "Fair enough. But don't think I've forgotten that you were the one who suggested that we study secrets in the first place. Anything you'd like to share?" She held up a hand. "I'm just putting it out there."

I couldn't help the smile that crept onto my face. My secret sat warm in my belly, as dizzying as the whiskey. I did not intend to share.

"What classes are you taking now?" she asked, seeing that a change of subject was necessary.

We let the conversation wander from school to old boyfriends to places we'd visited, our taste in movies, and trashy bands we'd genuinely liked back in the day. We ordered another round of drinks and sat there talking until well after ten o'clock.

"I told the babysitter I'd be back before eleven," I said at last. Sasha pushed away her empty glass and reached into her purse for cash. "This has been fun, Amy. Let's do it again sometime."

"My husband will be home by the end of the semester, so I won't have to get a sitter at the last second." I smiled at the thought of Marcus coming home. What would he think of Sasha?

"One question," I asked as we were leaving. "That guy who asked you to be his first wife. Did you think about it?"

"What, bossing all the younger wives around and throwing parties and getting my way all the time?" Sasha laughed. "Not for a second."

I laughed too. She would have made a pretty good first wife, I thought. She'd have kept everyone in line.

"I imagined it, though," she said. Her eyes were still bright, but there was something wistful in her features. "I mean, what an adventure."

Sasha gave me an appraising look to see if I understood, and I did. The idea of a wildly different life, even if it wasn't one you really wanted, could be hypnotizing.

• • • •

After three needle aspirations, my hematoma had almost vanished, leaving a lumpy scar in its wake. I would have to show The Doctor at our next appointment.

My semester workload increased, and the kids' schedules kept up their frantic pace. Since the urgency had faded now that there was only the scar to worry about, I stopped scheduling appointments for a few weeks. The Doctor had agreed that this was reasonable, and had promised to call periodically to check in on me, but I hadn't heard from him in a while.

I finally had a few days that weren't overloaded, so I called the hospital to schedule one last follow-up. As the phone rang I pictured The Doctor: his easy presence, his kindness, his attention, his flirtation, his touch, his kiss . . .

The nurse who answered took my name and information. "And what can I do for you today?" she asked. I was glad I hadn't gotten Cecil.

"I'd like to schedule one more follow-up. I just want to make sure that I'm, you know, healing normally." I cursed myself for stumbling over the words.

The nurse didn't notice. "What day did you have in mind? Colonel Williams has a few appointments open next week."

"COL. Williams isn't my usual doctor," I said, trying to sound casual.

"Let me take a look at your records. Oh, there, I see. I'm afraid your usual doctor isn't seeing patients now. For the time being, COL. Williams can see you."

I pulled the phone away from my ear and stared at it for a moment in disbelief.

"Amy?" said the nurse's voice.

"I'm here," I said. "Thank you for your help; I'll have to call back." I hung up before she could ask why.

Chapter Fourteen

I emailed The Doctor that afternoon.

I tried to make an appointment. They said you weren't there. Are you okay?

I wasn't sure what else to say. It wasn't normal for him to be silent for so long. Maybe he wanted to cut things off with me. I could think of a dozen reasons why that might be, and in that case I wasn't going to chase after him. On the other hand, it didn't seem like him to vanish without a word. Something must be wrong, and I wanted to help him if that was at all possible. I owed him that.

The more I thought about it, the more worried I became. Rather than write down every single concern that spun through my brain, I settled on the short message, and hit send.

And waited.

And waited.

But nothing came.

• • • •

The end of the spring semester was a bit like the arrival of winter break. The kids' schedules picked up, finals and final projects crept in, and I was constantly on the go. It was almost a shock, in the middle of all of this, when Marcus's return date arrived.

In the past whenever Marcus returned from deployment, I had the house spotless, his favorite dinner in the oven and two more in the fridge waiting for him, the kids freshly washed and dressed. This time, the kids and I cleaned frantically down to the last minute, and there had been no time to plan and prepare a special dinner.

When Marcus walked in, we all dropped what we were doing and raced to where he stood. This time there was no shyness from the kids. The twins shrieked their joy as Marcus lifted them in turn and spun them around in a wide circle. Margie clamped onto his leg, and Lydia opted to climb him jungle-gym style. Even Conrad, who was still wrestling with how to be cool, presented his hand for a high five.

I waited until the screeching of voices subsided before pushing my way through to receive a hug. We held each other close for a full thirty seconds, just feeling the steady warmth of each other, before pulling back enough to kiss. Marcus's touch held the same slow-burning heat it always had, and for a moment I seriously considered banishing the children to their rooms and dragging Marcus to ours.

Instead, I stepped away. "Are you hungry?"

Marcus laughed. "I could eat a bear." He detached Margie from his leg and swung her up onto his shoulders, growling like the bear in question. Margie giggled.

It was always strange to hear his voice on that first day back, so familiar after being absent so long.

"We're going to have to do takeout tonight," I said apologetically. "I'll make it up to you this weekend, I promise, but I didn't have a chance to go grocery shopping."

If this startled Marcus, it was only for a minute. "I'm happy with whatever's in front of me as long as I get to eat it with my family." He leaned down toward Margie conspiratorially. "Especially if it's a bear," he growled, and tickled her until she collapsed.

Lydia howled with laughter, and Alice presented herself to be tickled next.

• • • •

As always, I was glad to have Marcus back in our home—and our bed. In some ways this homecoming was like any that had come before. We had a chance to reinvent our family, rediscover our familiar habits, and revisit our desire for each other, the pleasures of our shared life made that much sweeter after having been apart so long.

This time, though, the rest of our lives had moved on in the meantime. Usually after Marcus returned, the rest of us felt disoriented for a few days. When the kids had been younger and we'd spent most of our days at home, Marcus had almost felt like an intruder in our private world. He'd been a welcome intruder, of course, but we'd had to work to fit him in.

That was not the case this time. The hole left by his absence had shifted and settled and taken on a shape that wasn't familiar to him. This was, in part, because the kids were old enough to remember Marcus, and warmed to him much more readily. The real change, though, was in our focus. When we'd all spent our days at home, Marcus's presence had disrupted our gravitational force, altering our orbits. This time, life sped on.

I was able to make us a fancy dinner on Saturday, but that meant that I had to spend Sunday evening catching up on my studies. The next day, Marcus came in to find the rest of us in the living room for our usual evening homework session.

"It's almost six," he observed.

"I know," I said.

"When do you want to eat?"

I glanced up from my book. "I'll start dinner as soon as I'm done." Marcus nodded, and it occurred to me that in the old days I had insisted that dinner be served at exactly six every night. I'd been almost tyrannical about it.

"I've gotten a little more lax about timing lately," I said. The words sounded like an apology, but I didn't feel apologetic. I was doing what worked. The kids certainly appreciated the new, less rigid version of my parenting style.

"I can start dinner," Marcus offered. He stood there for another moment. "It's nice to see you all in here working together."

He left us, and a few minutes later I heard the clatter of pans.

It must have been disorienting to come home from his shortest-ever deployment and find his home so fundamentally changed. I hoped he'd get used to the way things were now, even grow to enjoy them. I knew I had.

• • • •

To celebrate the end of the semester, we invited Kari and Raife over for a cookout. It would be a chance to socialize without any of the social pressures involved with hosting a larger gathering.

When they got out of the car, the first thing I noticed was how much bigger Kari's belly had gotten. I reached down unconsciously to touch my newly tight abdomen. Only a few years ago I'd been pregnant too, although it felt like a lifetime ago.

"You're looking great," I said, kissing her on the cheek. "Are you ready for round two?"

Kari nodded, then paused, then shook her head. "Sort of. Maybe. At least this time I have some idea of what to expect."

"Come sit down," said Marcus. "There are burgers on the grill."

Kari passed Yasmine to her husband for the walk to the backyard. "Do you ever get used to this?" she muttered to me.

"Just in time to actually have the baby," I told her. "Then you have to get used to being normal-sized again."

"As always, your comfort is a balm," said Kari, rolling her eyes.

We settled on the porch where we sipped cool drinks and watched the kids run rampant in the yard. Yasmine was just getting the hang of walking on her own, and Margie and Lydia entertained her. I enjoyed watching our children play together. I caught Kari doing the same, and we shared a smile.

"So, how's being back?" Kari asked my husband.

Marcus lifted the lid of the grill and flipped a burger. "It's great. I mean, it's always great. This time in particular." He looked at me as if searching for a response, and I smiled.

There was a lot that he didn't say, a lot he never said. Whatever had happened on this last mission was really getting to him, but that wasn't the kind of baggage he would unload on me even if he wasn't under oath. I was grateful for this, although I knew it must be hard on him. Truthfully, I wasn't sure if I could handle hearing about what he'd been through.

Raife nodded, clearly sensing whatever was going on for Marcus and hoping to route it with chatter. "I get it, man. I tell you what, the first thing I want when I get back is always a burger." He winked at Kari. "Well, okay, the *second* thing I want is a burger."

I snickered, and Kari smacked his shoulder.

"Well, here are the burgers," said Marcus grandly, his expression unguarded again. He flipped them expertly onto a platter and set them in the middle of the table. The kids came tumbling in across the lawn, and we helped ourselves to patties, buns, and cheese.

It was a pleasant way to spend an afternoon, with no worries and no pressures, the semester's assignments behind me and the summer stretching wide and vacant before us. Not so long ago my whole life had been like this, centered around social gatherings and my children's schedules, Marcus's work, and the house. For years, summer had been just more of the same, except with day camps and occasional vacations in place of after-school activities.

For years, every day had looked pretty much like every other, and that was fine.

Until one day it wasn't.

• • • •

Three weeks after I sent my initial email, I finally texted The Doctor. *Did something happen? Is everything okay?*

I received no answer that day.

Or the next day.

Or the next.

• • • •

Sasha called me a week after the end of the semester.

"Are you free Wednesday evening? I want to celebrate summer by exercising my right to make plans on a weeknight."

"Let me check with my husband," I told her. "I'll see if he can watch the kids that night."

"That's right," said Sasha. "Your husband is back. Well, let me know what he says."

She said this with relative indifference, and I realized that she had never met Marcus. She hadn't factored him into my life at all. Everyone I'd known for years—even The Doctor—had either known him or known of him. Most people knew me as Marcus's wife, or as the mother of one of my kids. To Sasha, though, I was just Amy, the person she'd worked with once in class.

"You should meet him sometime," I told her. "You'd like each other."

"Then I'll pick you up on Wednesday, if you're coming," she said. "I'll stop in before we leave, okay?"

"Perfect," I said. "I'll let you know."

• • • •

Alice and Eliza had insisted on lying in bed with Marcus for their bedtime readings every night since his return. I enjoyed watching the three of them together while Marcus read their books in silly voices or tried to remember the words to Mother Goose rhymes. When they fell asleep we would each carry one back to their bed in the next room.

Then, at last, we had a little time to ourselves. I felt safe with his arms around me, warm with his legs between mine, and loved when his hands stroked my back or smoothed my hair. This short time before we fell asleep was the only point in the day that we were able to give each other our full attention.

"We should take the kids to the beach soon," said Marcus as we settled in. "I bet they're missing the water."

"I'll look into it," I said, and then suddenly remembered Sasha's call. "Do you mind watching the kids on Wednesday night? Sasha wants to go out."

"Sure, I'm happy to. Who's Sasha?" asked Marcus, frowning as if he was trying to remember what she looked like.

"From my class last fall, remember?"

"Oh." He nodded. "Sorry, forgot the name. Are you having a girls' night?"

"We'll probably have a drink or two. Nothing too out of control." I smirked. "Unless we're feeling crazy."

"Then people had better stay out of your way," said Marcus gravely.

"Yeah," I said. "I'm trouble."

He grinned.

I snuggled closer and kissed him deeply, and he held tight to me.

"I missed you," I told him. "I'm glad you're home."

He shook his head, then pressed his forehead to mine. "I love you, Amy," he whispered. His voice was deep and husky.

I ran my fingers across the slope of his jaw. "I love you too," I breathed.

He slid his hands up my thighs and left a trail of little kisses tingling across my throat. "Care to show me how much you missed me?"

"I don't know," I teased. "I missed you a lot. I wouldn't want to overexert you."

His hands roamed higher and we didn't speak again.

• • • •

Sasha arrived at seven thirty.

"Nice to meet you, Marcus," she said, shaking his hand. This done, she sailed past him into the living room and settled on the couch. Marcus blinked at her, bemused by this woman he'd never met who felt so at ease in his own home.

"So, Amy says you met in class?" he asked.

"We had an assignment together last fall."

There was silence.

"I hear you're recently back from deployment," Sasha said at last.

"A couple of weeks ago, yeah," said Marcus.

More silence. These two people, I realized, had nothing in common but me.

"Well, should we get going?" Sasha asked me.

"Yeah," I said, "I think so. I'll be back by eleven, okay?" I gave Marcus a quick kiss and grabbed my bag.

Marcus nodded his agreement and waved us off. I wondered if he regretted pushing me to get out more, to start classes, to spend more time on myself.

It wasn't bad, but it was different. We both had some adjusting to do.

• • • •

I texted The Doctor, *I'm worried. Are you okay?*

He did not reply.

• • • •

On the first Sunday in June, I laced up my sneakers, pulled my hair back, and drove to the park I passed on my way to the hospital. The sun hadn't risen yet. It was warm already, but it would be cool in the shade of the trees. I'd packed water and some trail mix.

Every Sunday morning, rain or shine, The Doctor had said.

It was time to go hiking.

Chapter Fifteen

I had been right—it was pleasant under the trees.

I hadn't realized how many trails there were in the park. Driving by, it had never struck me as very large. Now, on foot, I realized that the park mostly ran away from the road, and that while there was a network of main trails used by day hikers and cyclists, smaller footpaths crisscrossed between them like arteries. I'd expected to walk down the trail and run into The Doctor at any moment, but I now saw that I could easily spend the whole day here and not even walk on the same paths he had, much less stumble across him.

I pulled out my phone and stared at the screen for a moment, wondering if I should text him. I wasn't entirely sure what I would say. Instead, I stuffed it in my pack and headed off in search of him.

At first I stayed focused on the people I passed. There were plenty of people on the main trails. Most of them were lean joggers in brightly colored workout clothes and expensive sneakers, but others walked in groups of two or three, out for a casual morning expedition. Statistically speaking, I was looking for a needle in a haystack, and I didn't want to risk missing him. I could only hope that he still came out here to hike. After about half an hour, though, my attention wandered to the surroundings. In spite of all the people out on the trails, the park felt private. The cars out on the highway sounded far away, overwhelmed by birdsong and the rustle of branches above me as a little breeze blew through. Dappled sunlight fell through the canopy, warm across my shoulders. Even the air smelled cleaner.

I could understand why The Doctor liked this.

I pulled out my phone again and typed, *You said every Sunday. I'm hiking. Are you?*

It occurred to me that I might as well turn back, but by then I was enjoying the hike for its own sake. I felt awake, alert, and in no particular rush. It was good to be on my own. I didn't have to answer to anyone.

My phone chimed with an incoming text, and I scrambled for it. Of course it might be someone else, an unrelated message.

But it was him.

All it said was, *Front entrance in 10.*

I whipped around and joined the joggers in a brisk trot back toward the parking lot.

• • • •

The Doctor was sitting on a bench when I arrived. He was looking off toward the road, but as if he could feel my eyes on him, he turned toward me and met my gaze. I couldn't keep myself from smiling. As I approached, I could see how warm his expression was, and I felt a profound sense of relief. I wanted to grab him, wrap my arms around him, greet him with a passionate kiss . . .

I slowed my pace and realized that I wasn't sure how to greet him. We'd never run into each other off of hospital grounds. What should

I do with all these other people coming in and out of the park only a few feet away?

I could see my own uncertainty mirrored on his face. He gave me a wave and rose from the bench. I realized with a jolt of surprise that his right arm was held in a sling.

"Let's take a side path," he suggested by way of greeting. "We can talk privately."

I nodded my agreement, and he headed off to the head of a small footpath, with me trailing just behind.

We walked in silence for a few minutes. The path was hemmed in more closely by trees than the main thoroughfare, and although we couldn't have been more than a few dozen yards from the hikers and joggers, we felt decidedly alone.

"Are you okay? What happened to your arm?" I asked at last. "I've been worried about you."

"Dislocated shoulder." He indicated the sling. "It needs at least six weeks to heal, but they won't let me back in the OR until fall."

I winced. "Ouch. What were you doing?"

"Racquetball," he sighed. "I overextended it. Not even an exciting story, just a freak accident."

"So what about work? I tried emailing. I tried texting. The hospital couldn't tell me anything."

"I've been moved over to teaching for the semester," he said bitterly. "I wasn't much use in the operating room with one hand."

"I'm sorry to hear that," I told him.

"Thanks."

"You could have told me, you know. I was really worried about you." I let out my breath and looked up at the trees. "Relationships are give and take. If you need anything, or you want someone to listen, you know that you can trust me."

"I'm sorry," he said, and I could hear the sincerity in his voice. Did he notice that I'd called what we had a relationship? It sounded strange to me, but I wasn't sure what else to call this thing between us.

I sped up my pace to circle in front of him, stopping him in his tracks. "Everything's going to be okay," I told him. "You are okay. Okay?"

He gestured fiercely to his shoulder. "I feel useless. I can't work, it takes forever just to get dressed in the morning, I'm in constant pain, and I don't know how long this will take to recover. And . . . and I was taking care of you. You aren't fully healed, and I can't do anything right now."

"It's a temporary injury," I said. "You need to focus on yourself. I don't need you to take care of me. I like it, but I don't need it."

"Like it but don't need it?" He laughed suddenly, then pulled me close and kissed my forehead. "Is that how you feel about me?"

I made a big show of thinking this over, and his smile widened.

"Just don't disappear again," I said as we resumed our walk.

"I won't," he answered, and he put his good arm around me. "I promise."

• • • •

Marcus was at his weekly basketball game, which usually ran late into the night, especially if they stopped by the bar for a beer afterward.

That week, basketball night was accompanied by a thunderstorm. Once I was sure that the kids' lights were off, I headed to the wine rack and reached for a bottle and a glass. I took my phone out of my pocket—it was too late to call Kari, and I wasn't in the mood to talk to anyone else.

Warm rain sprayed off the porch cover, spattering tiny drops against my legs as I sat down in one of the folding Adirondack chairs. The breeze was warm enough that a bit of water on my feet didn't matter. I kicked off my shoes and shoved them toward the door, dangling my bare toes over the edge of the porch. I kept my mind clear as the wine relaxed me—no school, no Marcus, no Doctor, no kids.

I enjoyed these moments I got to spend with myself, thinking about nothing and no one.

• • • •

Friday night, Marcus took me to dinner at our favorite Chinese restaurant in the city. The kids stayed home with the sitter, who was beginning to enjoy regular employment at our house.

I took my time getting ready. I'd been looking forward to the date since Marcus suggested it. We had a lot to celebrate with his safe return, and I wanted him to know how happy I was to have him home. When I stepped out of our room wearing a dress that was cut to hug my curves and showcase my legs, the slow sweep of Marcus's gaze across my body told me how much he appreciated it.

At the restaurant, we ordered our favorite dishes, a few drinks, and spent the evening talking, laughing, and sharing meaningful looks across the table. It amazed me that he could still make me feel like no one else in the world existed. His stare was the same as it had been when we first met, and in one glance he could make me feel wanted, needed, and loved. I was glad to have him completely to myself, if only for a few hours.

As we waited for the dessert, Marcus reached across the table to take my hand. "The unit is having a dinner next Tuesday," he said. "Can you arrange for the sitter?"

"I'll ask her when we get home." I tried not to wince. "And I suppose I should ask her if she's free for the ball, too?"

"Good thinking," said Marcus, leaning back to make room as the waiter brought our desserts.

I hadn't thought of the upcoming military ball since the first time Marcus mentioned it, mostly because I dreaded attending. Of all the military functions, balls left me feeling the most wrong-footed, the most out of place. They were the sort of event that women like Tanya May and the general's wife loved—everyone dressed in their finest, dancing and chatting politely and following all the rules of military etiquette.

We took our time walking hand-in-hand back to the car, did some window shopping, people-watching, and paused to watch a street artist sketch. Sometimes—less and less often these days—I missed Hawaii's beaches and balmy weather, but the liveliness of the big mainland cities was worth the trade.

While Marcus fished in his pocket for change to drop into the artist's cup, I checked my phone to see if the babysitter had called. No call, but two emails. The first was from The Doctor, and the second was from Professor West, my research analysis professor from the previous fall, who'd taught the class where I met Sasha.

The email had been sent to about a dozen recipients and was titled Research Opportunity.

Dear All,

As a result of your excellent work over the last year, I have recommended you for a new research position beginning this fall. This project will count as an accredited academic study. An informational night will be held next Tuesday in my office at 5pm. As this project will commence with the upcoming fall semester, enrollment paperwork must be filed as soon as possible. Thank you, and I look forward to seeing you there!

Sincerely,

Dr. Bannon West

"Interesting," I murmured. I scrolled up, then scanned the list of recipients. Alina, Sasha, and Nurul had all received the email as well. I didn't recognize any of the other names, but that didn't mean much. I didn't know that many of my fellow students.

"What's interesting?" asked Marcus.

"One of my old professors emailed me," I said as we headed back to the car.

"What did he have to say?"

"It sounds like there's a new research project starting up in the fall. He wants some of us to help out, I guess."

He unlocked the car and we got in. "What kind of project?"

"Not sure," I said. "We'll find out more on Tuesday."

"What's on Tuesday?"

"He's having some kind of informational meeting."

Marcus shoved the key into the ignition but didn't start the car.

"What's wrong?" I asked.

"Next Tuesday is the dinner at work. I thought you'd be there."

"Oh." I frowned. "I'm sorry, but I'm not sure I can go now. This meeting's in the late afternoon."

"Then I'll let them know I'll be attending on my own." Marcus cleared his throat and turned the key.

I wasn't sure how to respond to the tone in his voice. He was upset and disappointed. I didn't want our date to end in an argument. Marcus and I had disagreed before, but we'd always been able to talk things out, even when it meant one of us deferring to the other. I didn't know how to fight with him over not being able to support him at a work event. This was a first for us.

Was I being selfish? Or was he?

"I'm sorry," I said under my breath.

"You always come to work dinners with me," said Marcus. He plowed on before I could form a retort. "I'm still figuring out how to adjust to you being in school. It's new for me. I'll make your excuses and tell everyone you'll see them at the ball."

"I will definitely be at the ball," I said. "Wouldn't miss a ball! You know how much I love them." I tried to lighten the mood with my teasing sarcasm, even though the car seemed to be shrinking around us, all the air forced out by the rising tension.

"You? Never." Marcus gave me a quick look followed by a smile. "I know how you feel about them, but . . ."

"But I know how much they mean to you." I rubbed my hand on the back of his neck, which I knew always calmed him when we had a disagreement. "I'll be good."

"You're better than good," he said and lifted one hand off the wheel for a moment to squeeze my thigh. "That's how we make this work, though, isn't it? We make sure that the other person is getting whatever they need. The dinner doesn't matter to me as much as school does to you."

"Thank you." I put my hand on his. "I love you."

"I love you too, Amy," he said.

I'd been wrong. We hadn't fought. The situation had only felt strange because, for the first time in our marriage, Marcus was the one who'd had to surrender ground.

It wasn't until after we'd gotten home, tucked the kids into bed, and Marcus had stepped into the shower that I remembered the second email, the one from The Doctor. It was short, only two lines long.

Thinking of you. Same time next Sunday?

I was still staring at it when my phone buzzed with a text from Sasha, asking if I planned to attend the meeting next week.

In the bathroom, Marcus turned off the shower. "Amy?" he called softly. "Are you still awake? Because if you're asleep, I'm gonna have to wake you up."

I smiled to myself and typed two quick messages. *Yes, see you Tuesday*, to Sasha. *Yes, see you Sunday*, to The Doctor.

"You won't have to," I called to Marcus as I powered down my phone. "I'm wide awake."

Chapter Sixteen

Sasha, Alina, Nurul, and a handful of people I didn't know were milling around in the hallway outside of Professor West's office. Nurul let out a squeak of excitement when she saw me and waved vigorously. Sasha greeted me with a hug.

"How have you been?" Alina asked, then went on without waiting for a response. "Do you have any idea what this is about? It can't be a coincidence that we were all invited. Professor West must have liked our project."

"Not everyone is from our class," Nurul observed. "I recognize a few people from the department events, though."

Professor West appeared at the far end of the hall, putting an end to our speculation. "Ah, good turnout! I'm glad so many of you could make it." He produced a key ring from his pocket and unlocked the office door, ushering us inside. An assortment of cheap plastic chairs had been set up ahead of time, and we shuffled in to claim our seats.

"So," said Professor West, perching on the edge of his desk and beaming at us. "I don't know if you've all met one another, but each one of you has taken a class of mine in the last year, and based on your work, I think you'll be excellent fits for this opportunity." He rubbed his hands together gleefully. "I'm doing research for a new book, and I'm looking for assistants that will be willing to carry out a series of interviews with the project's participants. If you're interested, we'll fill out independent study reports. As an added bonus, your names will be listed in the book as research assistants. It wouldn't hurt for resumes."

Sasha raised her hand. "What's the aim of the project?"

Professor West nodded excitedly. "We'll be looking at marriages, secrets, and why relationships break down. Those of you who are interested will help me develop questions, but the most important thing will be to build trust with the participants and get them to open up about their experiences. You can see why I thought your group would be a good fit." He beamed at Sasha.

This did sound like an excellent fit, and practical experience appealed more to me than sitting in a classroom.

"So you're looking exclusively at how secrets destroy marriages?" Sasha pressed.

"The other way around," said Professor West, spinning his pointer fingers together to demonstrate. "I'll be looking at why relationships fall apart, trying to diagnose what went wrong. Secrets may or may not be a factor. Ideally I'd like to speak with both partners of a failed relationship if possible, but I foresee problems with getting people to commit to that model . . ." He launched into an intricately detailed description of his project, but I was only listening with half of my brain.

On one hand, I found the project compelling. On the other, it reminded me of all that I stood to lose if my own secrets came to light.

Sasha leaned over. "Sounds like fun. Are you in?"

After a moment's hesitation I nodded. At the end of the meeting we headed to the front of the room and added our names and student numbers to the registration list.

Everyone else lined up after us to do the same.

• • • •

"So, are you taking advantage of the downtime away from the hospital?" I asked The Doctor. I had been trying to help him see the positive side of his situation. I could see for myself how hard it was for him to spend the summer out of surgery, and I couldn't imagine what he would do if he lost his position altogether.

"I'm not used to being home so much," he admitted. "My daily chore list is more exhausting than work. I'm not used to taking orders that involve detailed grocery lists or chauffeuring the kids from one event to the next. And the laundry!" He rolled his eyes dramatically. "It's endless, and then I have to *fold* it."

"Sorry, but I don't feel bad for you." I elbowed him playfully.

"Hey, hey, watch it!" He held his good arm out defensively. "I'm injured here. You should be gentle with me."

"I forgot that you were so delicate these days," I teased. "Do you want me to kiss it and make it better?"

The Doctor and I were now meeting regularly. Our second walk through the park had been pleasant, but I'd also been more aware of how close we were to the hospital. I could tell that he was nervous about running into a familiar face. This time, we'd decided to head into the city where we could disappear among the throngs of people.

"How about you? Anything exciting on the docket?"

"I'm going shopping this week," I said. "I'm getting involved with a research project through my department, and it involves interviews. I want something a little more, I don't know, professional." I already had plans to go dress shopping with Kari, but having his eyes on me as I tried each outfit would be worth making time for a second shopping trip.

"I wish I could. I'm covering extra classes this week." He grinned. "And the *laundry* . . ."

"Laundry doesn't usually count as an excuse, but since you're folding one-handed, I'll accept it this time. Oh well. I was hoping to find something nice to wear *under* the outfits while I was out."

His eyes lit up. "In that case, if an extra opinion is needed I suppose I could make time between classes to view pictures and help guide your shopping choices."

"That's a thoughtful offer," I said. "Or maybe I'll just wear them the next time we meet."

The Doctor raised his eyebrows. "Don't make promises you don't intend to keep." He suddenly stood up straighter, then squinted at something across the road. I followed his gaze and realized that he was examining the marquee of a movie theater.

"Do you want to catch a matinee?" he asked.

I squinted too. "Is anything good playing?"

"Who cares? It's a matinee. The theater will be empty." He wiggled his eyebrows suggestively.

The suggestion made me feel like a teenager again. But wasn't that what our whole relationship was like? Our time together was a series of stolen moments that had to be hidden from everyone we knew.

"Dark and empty?" I asked. "By all means, let's get your mind off that shoulder of yours."

He held out his arm and waited for me to take it. "Follow me," he said, blue eyes twinkling, and I let him lead me across the road to the theater.

• • • •

"This is tragic," Kari complained, patting her belly. "I look like a watermelon with legs."

"So we'll find you a melon-colored dress," I said, shuffling through the racks of floor-length dresses that came in every color and size. "No problem."

Shopping for the military ball was like shopping for prom, except that you could afford something really nice this time, and if you turned up in something less than magnificent you'd lose more than your high school reputation.

"It's easy for you to say," said Kari, glaring at my waist. "You look better than you did in college. *I*, on the other hand, have the hips of an elephant."

I snorted and held out a sparkly green chiffon concoction that looked more like a dessert than a dress. "Yeah, but your boobs look amazing."

Kari rolled her eyes, but she accepted the compliment.

Some of the other wives, I knew, would turn up their noses at dresses bought off the rack, but Kari and I agreed that it was a waste to spend all the time and money it took to have a custom dress made when you could really only wear it once. God forbid you wear last year's dress to next year's ball.

"Surely we can find something in the maternity section," I said, hoping to placate my increasingly grumpy-looking best friend.

"Maybe."

"Or we could dress you in a triple-XL gown and just safety pin the bodice back," I quipped. Kari laughed.

She left me to see what her options were, and I promised to meet her by the dressing rooms so we could try things on together.

I took my time searching through the selection. It had been one thing to wear my saucy dress to The Coffee, but the military ball was a formal event. Besides, people wouldn't just be looking at me. I'd be on Marcus's arm, and whatever I did would reflect back on him. I needed to look respectable. I needed to look perfect.

That didn't mean I had to wear a shroud, though. I pulled out a handful of dresses in bright colors, mostly with scooping necklines, one with a dropped back.

Kari was waiting by the dressing room door, a few gowns bunched in her arms.

"Ready? Let's get this over with," she said with a tight smile. I could sense her nerves through her joking.

I tried a yellow dress, then immediately discarded it because the color made me look sallow. The next was a deep blue with a gathered waist—a little old-fashioned, but in a classic fifties movie star kind of way. That was just the sort of look that would make the older set nod their approval.

"Amy, I can't reach," said Kari's voice from the next station. She sounded like she was struggling. "My arms won't go that far."

After another few grunts, the door swung open, and I gaped.

The dress was white, printed with a small floral pattern in pale hues which were picked out with beadwork so the flowers glittered when she walked. It was a simple dress that did nothing to hide her belly, but it made her look young, almost childlike, and the accent colors against her complexion gave her a kind of glow.

"Do I look like a milkmaid?" she asked, frowning down at herself.

"You look the heroine of a Jane Austen novel," I told her. "It's beautiful, Kar."

She shook her head and gestured to my dress. "It's not like *that*. But I guess I'd have trouble pulling off that look, all things considered . . ."

I herded her back into the changing room and zipped up the back of the dress for her. I put my hands on her shoulders and turned her so that she faced the mirror.

"Kari," I said, "look at yourself. You're gorgeous."

Kari frowned and squinted into the mirror. I looked too, and was a little startled at what I saw in the glass. Kari appeared so soft and sweet, and I . . . I looked sexy. Chic.

I understood suddenly why I had never told Kari about The Doctor: she wouldn't have understood. She might have excused me, but she wouldn't have sympathized. She lived in my old world, the world of rules and order and public image. Maybe someday she'd be ready, and I'd tell her, and she'd get it, but not yet.

"I think this is the dress for you," I told her. "Don't you like it?"

She twirled a tendril of hair around her finger and smiled shyly into the mirror. "I think I do," she said.

• • • •

Military balls are white-tie affairs, and the only thing that matters more than appearance is tradition. The most tedious tradition, in my opinion, was the receiving line.

Supposedly participation in the receiving line was optional, although Marcus would never have dreamed of ducking out. We waited behind Raife and Kari until the adjutant announced their names, and they were off down the line, shaking hands and smiling. Marcus and I followed when our turn came. We walked past the endless line of officers and distinguished guests, shaking hands and making empty small talk. Did this ritual actually make anyone feel important?

Ahead of me, Kari looked like an expert, floating down the line in her pale dress. On both sides of the line, most peoples' grins were too wide and seemed plastered to their faces, but Kari wore her role so comfortably. So confidently. I almost envied her for it, but I no longer felt compelled to play that part.

The general and his wife stood at the end, and I felt my skin crawl when I shook his hand. I remembered the pass he'd made at me more than a year before. I had heard that his wife was on to his behavior, but her smile revealed nothing. He had the good grace not to meet my gaze.

Marcus and I drifted toward the dining room. I could tell that he was a bit tense, maybe due to the large crowd. I grabbed his hand.

"Do you feel okay?" I asked in a low voice.

He squeezed back. "I'm fine."

I leaned into him as we walked, reminding him that I was there for support. "I love you," I said under my breath as we approached the table.

He pulled out my chair for me. "You look beautiful," he murmured as I sat. "I love you too."

Still to come were the speeches, the ceremonies, the mournful silence for fallen soldiers, and the reserved facsimile of a party that would stretch well into the evening, full of passive-aggressive comments about dresses, children, spouses, and faith . . .

When the banquet finally ended, Marcus and I made our way around the hall. I found humor in the way he joked and made small talk with people neither of us really knew. He had always been a charmer. It was impossible not to be drawn to him. I shook hands with his coworkers and their spouses, his bosses, and a few of the soldiers that he'd been deployed with. The entire time, Marcus held onto my arm, squeezing just tight enough to remind me that he needed me.

When we'd finally spoken to everyone, I looked around for Kari, hoping to say good night before we left. I spotted her out on the dance floor snuggled close to Raife.

"Dance with me," I said to Marcus suddenly. "For one song."

He followed me out onto the dance floor and pulled me into him. In that moment, I didn't care about anyone else in that hall. Tonight was about Marcus.

The band played on, and I made myself comfortable in his embrace. I looked up and gave him a quick kiss on each cheek.

"Thank you for tonight," I said.

He bent down to my ear. "That dress looks amazing on you," he whispered. "But for the past hour or so, all I've been able to think about is taking it off."

The song ended, and he took my hand, finally leading me to the exit.

• • • •

Kari went into labor exactly three weeks after the ball, and Yasmine came to stay with us until the new baby was ready to come home. Yasmine was wary of her brother when she met him for the first time. She seemed to think that she might break him.

As I watched Kari with her children, I remembered what my life had been like when Conrad was a toddler, when Lydia had joined him, and then when I'd had three babies in my arms at once in addition to my toddlers . . .

"Do you miss it?" asked Marcus as we headed home, leaving the family alone with their newest member. "Having a baby, I mean?"

"Are you asking me if I want another one?" I teased. "Because I love our children, but I think we have enough."

Marcus smiled, but he sounded almost nostalgic when we spoke. "Don't you miss when they were small like that, brand new, before we knew who they were or what they liked, when we were the whole world to them?"

"I loved the kids when they were small," I told Marcus. "I love them now."

The thing was, I enjoyed spending time with the kids more now that they had their own inner lives, their own interests and personalities. Sure, they had been cute babies, but I appreciated being able to relate to my children.

Does he miss the days when I was like that? I wondered. When he'd been my whole world? When I clung to his arm and waved and smiled and never questioned the rules—much less broke them?

Chapter Seventeen

"What are you planning to do for your birthday, dear?" Corrina asked.

I shrugged my shoulder against the phone. "I haven't really thought about it."

It had been years since we'd done anything for my birthday—things had been too hectic or the kids had been too young or Marcus had been deployed. This year, for the first time in a long time, we weren't scrambling to get something done.

"Would you like to come visit?" I asked, bracing myself for her answer. She hadn't visited since she'd come to stay with the kids, and I had an uncomfortable feeling that she'd notice the changes in me if she came now. She had a nose for intrigue, and despite her tendency to put her own needs first, her perception was alarmingly acute.

"No, darling, I don't think I'll come. I had a much better idea. What would you say to spending your birthday at the beach?"

"Marcus had suggested a family vacation," I said. "I haven't had time to plan anything, though."

"I'd like to book you a spot in the Outer Banks. It's a bit of a drive, I know, but it's so beautiful this time of year."

"Oh, Mom. You really don't have to."

"Of course I don't *have* to," she said. "I want my family to enjoy themselves, Amy. Please let me send you somewhere nice for your birthday."

I had to admit, the idea of a few days on a boardwalk, eating pizza and wriggling my toes in the sand while my kids splashed in the surf sounded wonderful.

"Well, then thank you. I'll talk to Marcus about timing and let you know."

"You're welcome, love." Corrina blew a kiss into the phone before hanging up.

That night I told Marcus about my mother's beach birthday gift. The look on his face . . . that was the real present.

• • • •

"I told you the months would go by quickly."

We had met at a cozy coffee shop, which had become a regular meeting spot of ours, located on a remote side street on the harbor side of the city.

"Thanks to you, I've been well taken care of." The Doctor lifted his coffee mug and shook his head. "The only problem is that now I've been spoiled for hospital cafeteria coffee."

"I can smuggle some in for you," I offered.

"And I've been spoiled by being able to have you whenever I want." He leaned closer and slid one hand up my leg under the cover of the table.

I looked down at the hand that was creeping up my inner thigh. "Maybe I can arrange that as well."

The Doctor smiled.

"Seriously, are you anxious about going back to work?" I asked. "I know I would be."

"A little," he admitted. "I'm not sure what I'm walking into. But I want to go back. I need to go back."

"I'm excited for you." I leaned my head onto his shoulder. "Although I'll miss our time together." I lifted my cup to take a sip of my coffee, but there was only cold foam left at the bottom of the mug. We must have been sitting there for over an hour. It hadn't felt anywhere near that long.

"Amy." The Doctor moved his hand to my knee, the playfulness vanishing from his expression. "I don't know if I could have made it through this without you. Your conversations motivate me. Being near you calms and excites me at the same time."

I wrapped my arm in his and smiled.

The Doctor turned toward me until his mouth brushed my ear and whispered, "I'll think of you every day."

I rubbed my cheek against his for a few moments. "I already do," I said.

Nobody at the coffee shop knew who we were. Nobody thought twice when I leaned in to kiss him.

• • • •

"Are you almost packed?" asked Marcus.

"Almost." I looked up from my suitcase. "Why?"

"Because I wanted to show you something," said Marcus. He leaned against the doorway into our bedroom, his arms crossed, exuding an air of casualness that was definitely suspicious.

I narrowed my eyes at him. "What are you up to?"

"There's something outside." He jerked his thumb toward the front door.

He waved me through the door, then followed me toward the entryway. I pushed open the front door and gaped at the black two-door sport coupe parked in the driveway.

"What is this?"

"I couldn't let your mother upstage me now, could I?" He grinned. I tackled him in a hug and clung to his neck. "It's beautiful! Thank you!" I glanced over my shoulder toward the car. "One problem—the kids aren't going to fit in there."

"It really only seats two comfortably." He smiled, pointing toward himself. "I figured it was time you had something smaller and more stylish to get around in. Something that suits you better."

We'd been talking about getting a new car for months. I was usually the one who drove the minivan, and I was ready to trade it in. We'd gone back and forth about what would fit a family of seven. I'd tried to explain how I felt driving the van around, but I didn't think Marcus had been listening. The van was practical, he'd assured me. But this gesture made it clear that he was paying attention. The van might work for moving the kids, but this car was meant for me.

Marcus swung me around. "So you like it?"

"I *love* it!" I kissed him. "And I love you."

"I love you too." He hugged me back. "I'm glad you're happy. I like it when you're happy."

I pulled him tighter, nuzzling against his neck. "You make me happy," I mumbled into his shirt.

And it was true. He did make me happy.

A lot of things made me happy these days.

• • • •

The Outer Banks were just as beautiful as I remembered from my childhood vacations. When I pictured the beach, I thought automatically of Hawaii's white sands and crystal waters, with the reef sparkling far below. This beach was not tropical, but it *was* hot. There was something satisfying about the muggy heat, though. It made me appreciate the water that much more.

Marcus and Conrad raced along the edge of the surf, kicking up foam behind them. Someone's small dog hopped back and forth on the end of its leash yapping at them until Margie decided to befriend it. The other girls and I walked more slowly, letting the cold water wash over our ankles, tempering the heat.

I pulled out my phone to snap a quick picture of the kids along with a quick note: *Mom, thank you for this, best gift so far.*

The waves were nice, but the truly wonderful thing was to have my family around me. Sometimes the kids grew so fast, it was like I'd blinked and missed it. They had lives of their own now, and interests, and friends. In some ways we'd grown apart, but we were stronger as a family, especially with Marcus home. Everything felt so much more natural with him here. We were all happier when he was home.

"How's it going back here?" asked Marcus, jogging up again. "Are you ready for some lunch?"

"I want to go swimming," Lydia said, pouting.

Marcus jiggled her shoulder playfully. "You don't want a deep-dish pepperoni, huh? Huh?"

Lydia considered this offer. "Can we go swimming after?"

"Not for thirty minutes," said Marcus, pulling his lips into an exaggerated frown. Lydia giggled.

"Yeah, no swimming right after you eat or the *sharks* will get you!" cried Conrad.

"Sharks?" screeched Eliza. Margie immediately ran toward the water in hopes of making a new shark friend.

"There aren't sharks," said Lydia, scowling at her brother.

"Well, I'm ready to eat something," I said. "Then we can head back to the hotel to grab our suits. After that we can come out again without having to worry about the sharks or cramps or whatever it is that we're worried about."

We ambled back to the boardwalk, where Marcus let the kids pick what they wanted to eat. "What do you want, Amy?" he called back.

I raised my arms in a gesture that said, *I'll be fine with whatever you bring me.*

I found a table and waited for my family to return with pizza and hot dogs and icy, fizzy drinks. This wasn't the kind of thing we usually ate at home, but that was part of the fun of vacationing, wasn't it? You stopped worrying about all the things that bothered you and just let yourself relax.

On our way back to the hotel, Margie began to tell me a story about a boy from camp.

"Benny's really popular. All the girls think he's cute."

I raised my eyebrows. "Do they really?"

"The other girls took a vote and decided that he was the cutest boy at camp." She wrinkled her nose. "Mom? Can I wear a shirt over my bathing suit?"

"Sure, honey." I frowned at the change in topic. "Why do you ask?"

"Because Benny says I still have baby fat."

"Sounds to me like Benny still has a baby brain," I teased. "Who cares what he thinks?"

"Everyone cares."

"Why?"

"Well . . ." She chewed her bottom lip. "He's popular, I guess."

"Margie, honey, it doesn't matter what Benny thinks or what the girls think or what anyone else thinks. It only matters what you think."

"So I look okay in my bathing suit?" she asked.

"Doesn't matter what I think, remember?" I put my hand on her shoulder to stop her and turned her around, bending down so that we could meet each other's eyes. "I want you to feel comfortable. If you feel comfortable, then I'm happy."

"How do I make myself comfortable?" she asked, fidgeting with her flip-flop.

"Well to start with, you learn not to care so much about what other people want. If there's something that you can fix to make yourself feel better, fix that. Like braces, when your teeth aren't straight." I grinned, showing off my post-braces smile. "But if the problem is with what *other* people think, try making some new friends while the other girls are hanging around with the mean boys."

I kissed her forehead and stood up, taking her hand. The rest of our family was ahead of us now, and Marcus looked back to see what was holding us up. I waved, and he waved back.

"Mom?" Margie looked up at me. "Please don't tell Dad."

"I won't," I said. "For Benny's sake."

• • • •

Back in our hotel room, I picked out a bathing suit from the pile I'd jammed into my suitcase. Marcus was next door with the kids, organizing the changing process.

Was it true what I'd said to Margie, that the only thing that mattered was what we thought of ourselves? Or was that just what I wanted to teach my daughter to believe?

I took a moment to admire myself in the mirror before heading over to the kids' room. It wasn't often that I looked at my mostly bare body and reflected on the changes that it had gone through. The pregnancies, the weight fluctuation between each birth, the failed band, the surgeries. I was comfortable with myself now, dressed and undressed. I was at peace with my body—I looked good, and I felt good. So maybe it was true.

I smiled at myself in the mirror, looking over my body from the side, turning to a back view, then to the front, and pulled up short at the sight of my abdomen. Most of my belly was smooth and flat, but where the hematoma had once bulged out, now there was a little flap of skin and a patch of scar tissue, startlingly white against the skin around it. I pulled a U-turn and headed back to my bag.

"A one-piece, huh?" asked Marcus when I met the rest of them in the hall. He winked at me. "Too bad."

"To the beach!" insisted Lydia, and she led the charge back out toward the water. Margie skipped behind her, proudly wearing her new bathing suit.

I hung back, running my fingers over the flap of skin. Although the press of the bathing suit pushed the bulge flat, I could still feel it there.

Like I'd told my daughter, if something makes you uncomfortable, you either find a way to live with it or fix it.

It was the only time on the vacation that I thought of The Doctor.

• • • •

"Schedule a regular office appointment," The Doctor told me. "I'll take care of it."

Two weeks before the start of classes, The Doctor was cleared to return to the OR and to start seeing patients in the hospital again. I scheduled an appointment right away. The Doctor had explained to me that he was going to fix this but that he wanted to avoid bringing me back into the OR, as there was no record of my recent tummy tuck.

When I walked into his office now, he greeted me with a smile. "Are you ready?" he asked.

"I'm not sure what I should be ready *for*." I winked at him. "But if you're the one asking, then sure, I'm ready."

He helped me onto the paper-covered exam table and rolled up the edge of my camisole until the scar was visible. I was sorry that he'd put his gloves on already. The warmth of his touch would have been comforting.

"More needles," I said with a frown. "My favorite. Now you know why I keep coming back."

He laughed softly. "This is the last time, I promise."

"I've heard that somewhere before," I told him.

The Doctor sunk the tip of the needle into my skin while I tried not to flinch. "You should be good and numb. I told the anesthesiologist to give me the best he had." Within seconds, I was aware of a tingling sensation, which faded quickly and was replaced with only a dull pulse.

I caught his glance toward the door before he produced a scalpel. "If you feel anything, just tell me and we'll stop." He put his hand on my belly, pinching the flap of skin between his thumb and forefinger.

"Oh, I sure will." I waited for him to lift the scalpel. Was the anesthesia strong enough? I sure hoped it was.

"Amy?" he said. "You might not want to watch."

Obediently, I averted my face and stared at the ceiling, half closing my eyes against the too-white glow of the lights.

"Talk to me," I said. "Unless that will make it too hard for you to focus."

"Don't worry about my focus," he said. "All right, so I got an offer from an annual surgeon's conference. This fall they're holding it just a few hours away, and they've asked me to present."

"That's great!" I said.

"It's the biggest conference on the East Coast," he continued, obviously pleased by my enthusiasm. "The invitation is a real honor."

"You deserve it."

"This is a great opportunity, Amy. I'm looking toward retiring from the military, and this . . . this means that I've done something worthwhile with my career." He sat up straight in his chair. "Okay, that's done, I'm going to glue you back up now."

"Right," I said. "Retirement." What would that mean for us? Would he move? Would he have to find another job that didn't leave him time for me?

He patted my numb side. "There, all done. I'll put in a prescription for something to help with pain."

"I was promised there wouldn't *be* any pain," I joked, sitting up.

"I'll text you tonight to see how you're feeling." He rolled my camisole back down and helped me off the table.

He looked so much more at peace now that he was back to work. "It's nice to see you back in your element," I said. His confidence was still just as palpable, as if he'd never been away.

"Sunday morning?" he asked softly as he helped my gather my things. I nodded once and kissed him on the cheek before I left.

On my way out past the front desk, I waved to Cecil, who lifted one eyebrow as I passed. "I haven't seen *you* in a long time."

"Nor are you likely to see me again," I mumbled to myself under my breath. Then I turned toward him, smiling broadly. "Good-bye, Cecil!" I waved as I pushed through the door. Surprised, apparently, by the cheeriness of my greeting, he waved back. And then I was gone.

• • • •

On the way home, I pulled my new coupe into Kari's driveway. I hadn't called ahead, but I had hardly spoken to her in weeks. I missed her.

As much as I loved classes and the new lifestyle that had come with making new friends, I missed Kari. She'd been a big part of my life, even when we lived thousands of miles apart. It was a shame that we were starting to lose touch now that we shared a town.

When I knocked on the door, Kari's mother answered, the new baby cradled in her arms. I gave them both a gentle hug.

"They're sleeping," she whispered. "Yasmine and Kari."

"Good thing I didn't call, then." She let me in, and I closed the door softly behind me. "I wanted to bring by a present." I held up the bag in my hand as evidence. Inside were two necklaces with little beach-themed charms dangling from the chains, a seahorse for Kari, a dolphin for Yasmine, mementos from the Outer Banks.

"Would you like to come back later?" asked Kari's mother. "Or I can give it to Kari when she wakes up."

"That's fine." I set the bag on the coffee table. "I know she's busy."

"Would you like to hold Ebrahim?" She smiled down at him and nuzzled his cheek. "He wasn't tired, so we've been spending some time together."

I held out my arms and let her pass Ebrahim to me. He was so small, with wide and curious dark eyes that resembled Kari's. I rocked him back and forth, and softly kissed his forehead.

"He's a quiet one," Kari's mom whispered. "Yasmine, do you remember? She was a screamer. She always wanted attention."

"She still does," I said, but I kept my eyes on the baby. He wriggled into my arms and closed his eyes, kicking his legs until he got comfortable. I loved being able to have a conversation with my children, to give them advice when they asked me for it, to see them try and fail and get up and try again. They'd all started out like this, though—small, and blank as new paper.

"He's so precious," I murmured.

Kari's mother reached out. "I can take him, if you need to go."

"A little longer, if you don't mind," I said.

"Not at all. Gives me a moment to finish up in the kitchen." She left us in the living room, and a moment later I heard the sound of running water.

I leaned back on the couch and adjusted the baby so that he could be more comfortable. His little body lay across my belly, but I couldn't feel it. My side was still numb from where The Doctor had injected me with anesthetic.

Chapter Eighteen

"Excited?" asked Sasha.

I looked down at the list of questions in my hand. We'd bounced ideas back and forth through email, with Dr. West's guidance, and narrowed it down to twenty. Not all of the questions could be applied to each participant, so we'd be allowed to pick and choose as we liked and ask our own questions when the participants opened up to us.

"I think so," I said. "But who's going to want to answer these? I wouldn't want to tell a stranger . . ." I scanned the list. *"At what point did you sense that the relationship was beginning to fail?* Or, *Which one of you initiated the breakup or divorce?* That's not the kind of thing you tell someone you don't know. A licensed therapist, maybe, but not some student doing research for a book."

"Why not?" Sasha leaned back against the wall and fanned herself with the printout. "A stranger's the perfect person to tell. People want to talk about their problems, but they can't always open up to someone they see regularly. A stranger has no stake in the game. They're the perfect person to unload on."

I opened my mouth to argue, then remembered trying to tell Kari about The Doctor. Wasn't that exactly how I'd felt? Instead, I said, "Is that what you do?"

Sasha tilted her head.

"Open up to strangers, I mean."

"Doesn't everyone start out as a stranger?" she asked, giving me a lazy sidelong glance.

One of the other assistants poked his head out into the hall. "They're here. If you want to go into your rooms and get set up, we'll send them in one at a time."

Sasha nodded to him, then gave me a little wave. "See you in a few."

I waved back before heading into my own room.

We had taken over a series of research offices for the first round of interviews. I took a seat in the chair closest to the window and tried to get comfortable. In the other room, Sasha was probably lounging in her chair, looking effortlessly in charge, confident that whoever walked through the door would find her instantly trustworthy and spill their secrets into her lap. I sat up straighter and crossed my ankles. Maybe it was better to channel my officer's wife persona, cool and unflappable, pleasantly remote. I read through the questions to refresh myself until the first participant arrived.

The man who stepped through the door was tall and well-built. He looked surprisingly . . . normal. I wasn't sure what I'd been expecting.

"Hello," I said, rising to greet him with a handshake. His grip was firm but clammy. "I'm Amy."

"Manny," he said gruffly, then cleared his throat. "Sorry. I'm a bit nervous."

My military persona wasn't designed to help put grown men at ease. I decided to try a more motherly approach. "If you aren't comfortable, I won't push you."

Manny shook his head. "I'm fine."

As he took a seat, I wondered if there was a reason that Sasha and I had been assigned to work with the male participants in the study. I'd assumed that it was because there were simply more female students so we had to be split up unequally, but maybe Sasha was on to something with her theory about trust. Was it easier for men to open up to an unfamiliar woman? Maybe they saw us as less threatening than another man.

"You know I'm going to record this, right, Manny?" I asked, holding up the slim silver device that the department had furnished for the interviews.

"We went over the paperwork before I came in."

"Perfect. So, Manny, are you married?"

"Separated."

"Can you tell me why you and your wife chose to separate?"

"It was my fault. I just . . . I felt stuck. I wasn't satisfied. I mean, I was happy, but . . ." He waved his hands helplessly. "Maybe you're too young to understand this, but you reach a point where you realize that no matter what happens, your life is more than half over. All the things that I'd worked for—the career, the family, the house—every new thing I got just meant losing something else."

I nodded but didn't press him.

"I'd been married to the same woman for almost thirty years. And I love Angie. But I started to realize that nobody would ever fall in love with me again, and that was terrifying." He let his eyes wander to the ceiling, clasping his hands tightly in front of him. "I just wanted a change. People looked at me and they saw Manny—oh, you know

Manny, he's older, he's a little out of shape, he's successful but boring, he's completely predictable. He doesn't take risks."

"So you decided to take one?"

"Her name was Marta. We met at work. She was young. Young enough to be my daughter, I know. It wasn't like that. I took her out. I bought her jewelry. I admired her. She has a boyfriend, she doesn't want an old man like me. She was using me. I'm not stupid, Amy. She thought she was leading me on, but she didn't know that I was already getting what I wanted. The secret. People looked at me and they thought they knew everything about me, but they didn't."

"What did your wife say when she found out?"

"She never found out about Marta. But then, after Marta called it off, I started going on chat rooms. Dating sites. Eventually, Angie caught on. She asked for a separation. She agreed to go to counseling, but I don't think she'll ever understand. That life, the one where people see you as typical? Normal? That's all that matters to her. Appearances. What people will say. She has still never asked me why I did this."

"And why did you?"

Manny rubbed his hands through his hair. "Angie's right. I was selfish. But sometimes you need to do something for yourself or you'll never figure out how to be happy."

"And are you happy now?"

Manny searched my face. I wondered if he thought I was judging him. "I don't know. The strange thing is, doing something for myself felt good, but I don't know if I ended up any happier than I was before."

• • • •

In the fifteen minutes between interviews, I went across the hall to check on Sasha.

"How are you holding up?" she asked.

I shook my head. "People do things for the oddest reasons."

"What, did you think everyone was as perfect as we are?" She grinned at me and leaned back in her chair.

I laughed. "Of course not."

"People don't know what they want. They think they do, but they don't."

"I know." I ran my fingers over my hair, smoothing it. "But we try to be perfect, don't we?"

"We try to look perfect," scoffed Sasha. "It's not the same thing."

• • • •

"I'd been married for twelve years. We have two kids together. After the first came along, the passion slowly died." Jamal cleared his throat. "After the second was born, it was gone."

"Did your physical intimacy end altogether?" I was relaxing into the clinical dispassion of interview questions, which made it easier to get more personal.

"Pretty much. I got bored." Jamal lowered his head. "I never thought I would stray from Sonia. I didn't plan to. But Kelsey was always so flirty and friendly. One day, I crossed the line and gave in to her."

"Where did you meet Kelsey?" I asked.

"The gym."

"And what happened with Kelsey?"

"We never slept together," said Jamal, his shoulders tensing defensively. "We just talked. Emails. Pictures. Texts. Sometimes it was just talk about how our days had gone. Other times it got more, you know, descriptive."

"Descriptive?"

Jamal rubbed the back of his neck. "We talked about what we'd like to do to each other. Sexually. The thing is, it wasn't about Kelsey. She could have been anyone. It was mostly about what was going on in my own head."

"How long did it last?"

"A year, maybe. Sonia got suspicious eventually, and she went through my phone. She found everything. Our entire relationship, all the messages and photos. She contacted Kelsey, and I never heard from her again." Jamal sat up straighter. "I know this sounds backward, but I still resent Sonia for causing that to end."

I looked down at my hands, where they lay folded in my lap. "You said it wasn't really about Kelsey. Did you just need the emotional connection?"

"It wasn't that emotional. Like I said, nothing ever happened. It just made me feel really wanted. Sonia hadn't wanted me for a long time."

"And Sonia left after she found out."

Jamal shrugged. "Not right away. We tried to work it out, but there wasn't much of a marriage left to save."

• • • •

This interview had run a bit over time. I went across the hall to stretch my legs and get a drink of water from the cooler. I didn't judge Manny or Jamal for what they'd done, but I didn't quite relate.

Sasha was chatting with another student beside the water cooler. "Hey, Amy. We're trying to figure out why happy people set themselves up to become unhappy by cheating."

I poured a paper-cupful of water and shrugged while I sipped it. I had no answers for them.

• • • •

"Since Deanna left me, I question myself every day," Vincent said. He was tall and thin, bald but attractive enough. He looked like he biked or swam. He was handsome, I supposed, but his broken heart was written all over his face.

"Do you blame yourself?"

"It's hard not to ask myself what's wrong with me. What does he have that I don't? I was her best friend, her lover, her provider, her protector. And she left anyway."

"Why do you think it's your fault that she had an affair?"

Vincent seemed to fold into himself. "I keep trying to understand. If I loved her so much, why did she need someone else? I should have paid more attention." He rubbed one eye with his palm. "It's my fault she was lonely."

Vincent was a victim of the affair, but I wondered if Deanna was a victim of the marriage.

"How did you find out about it?" I asked.

"She told me. She said she wasn't happy, and that the way for her to be happy was to leave. I begged her to stay, but she'd already moved on."

He looked so sad that part of me wanted to give him a hug, while the other half of me wanted to shake him and tell him it was time to let go. "How about you?" I asked instead. "How are you coping? Have you moved on?"

"I want to, but I don't see how I can." Vincent stared down at his shoes, his lips pinched. "I want answers. What did he offer that was so much better? Did she ever feel guilty? Was he ever in my home? In my bed? What else don't I know? Does she feel any regret over how she treated me?"

I cut in. "If she did feel regret, would you take her back?"

"In a heartbeat. And I'd be a better husband to her, having been through all this." He looked up at me again. "So in answer to your question, no, I have not moved on. She was *the one*, you know?"

Is there really only one person for everyone? Only one? How could one person fulfill all of another's needs completely?

That was the idea of marriage, though, wasn't it? To have and to hold until death do you part. Was Manny unreasonable? Jamal? Deanna? Or was that promise of forever the unreasonable demand?

You could love someone from the day you met them until the day you died, I was sure of that. But how could you close your heart off forever and swear, through sickness and in health, never to let anyone else in?

• • • •

On the next break, Sasha stepped through the door again and leaned back on it, examining me thoughtfully. "Tell me something, Amy. All these people that we've talked to today. Their hearts are broken. They're coming apart at the seams. Is it worth it?"

"Marriage? Absolutely."

"You didn't even think about it."

"Mine is," I said. "I've thought about it, and it is. I love Marcus. I love being a wife and a mother."

I'd always seen Sasha as a little aloof, a little cool, but for a split second I realized how she must see me. She saw me as trapped in a cage, but it wasn't like that. My marriage was a blessing, not a curse. Given the opportunity to start fresh, I'd still pick Marcus. I'd still pick my family. I'd give them my heart, every time.

My whole heart.

Wouldn't I?

• • • •

"I married for love," Charles said. "If you looked at our lives, you'd have said that everything was perfect. The house. The neighborhood. Our kids were honor roll students and star athletes."

"What was your wife like?" I asked.

"Clara was kind. Smart. Popular." His face softened when he spoke about her. "I always did what was expected of me. We were predictable. We were safe."

"And how did your affair begin?"

"I'd been wondering for a while if our lives were ever going to change. Or was this it? And if it's as good as it's going to get, was that good enough?"

"This was before you'd met anyone else."

"Yes. I wasn't really looking for another person, but for another side of myself. And when I met Trudy, it wasn't because I wanted to replace Clara. I was turning my back on who I'd become in my marriage."

"And how long did the affair with Trudy go on?"

Charles examined his hands. "After the first time, I tried to cut it off with her. It didn't work. The harder I tried not to think about her, the more I wanted her."

I could understand the feeling. "You were lured by the forbidden." He didn't correct me. "How did Clara find out?"

"Trudy and I told her together." Charles sighed. "I felt guilty about hurting Clara. That was never my intention. But I'm happier now. More myself. And Trudy and I are very much in love."

"Had you ever thought about leaving Clara before the affair?"

"The affair was my self-discovery. I needed to find the parts of myself that I'd lost."

"Thank you, Charles." I reached to turn off the recorder, then put it back, still running. "One more question. Do you think that there's one person for everyone? Was Clara the wrong person for you?"

He shook his head, his mouth twisting into a wry smile. "I think that people agree to be right for each other. You do your best to make the relationship work, and it either does or it doesn't. You can only do that with one person at a time, though, or you risk hurting everyone."

I shook his hand, then turned off the recorder at last.

• • • •

By the end of the fourth interview, my head was spinning. I was gathering my things when Sasha knocked.

"We're done for the day," she said. "A few of us are going to dinner later. Interested?"

"I'll have to run home first," I said, looking at my phone. "I'd like to change, and Marcus has a basketball game tonight. I'll have to call the sitter."

"We'll be there for a while. The place we met before, remember? Callahan's. I don't know about you, but after this I could use a drink."

"Sounds good." I shrugged the strap of my bag over my shoulder and headed out.

• • • •

"What do you do at these girls' nights out, anyway?" Marcus asked while I changed. The babysitter had arrived a few minutes ago and was entertaining the kids in the yard.

"Secret girl things," I teased. "Mostly we gossip about shoes and babies and handbags . . . same things you and the guys talk about at basketball, right?"

Marcus laughed.

I relented. "We talk about the project, mostly." I crossed to where he sat on the bed and leaned down to kiss him deeply. "Zip me up?"

He groaned. "Do I have to?"

"I don't want to be any later then I already am, and you have to get ready," I scolded. "But I might need help unzipping it later."

Marcus kissed my cheek, then let his shoulder rest against mine. "Sometimes I feel like I'm losing you. I know it's selfish, after encouraging you to spend more time on yourself."

"You aren't selfish," I promised. "I miss you sometimes too. But I'm right here. I've been here the whole time." And I kissed him again to prove it.

We pulled out of the driveway at the same time, heading in different directions. He honked and waved at me as he drove away.

While the GPS chirped directions to Sasha's favorite stomping ground, my mind wandered over the interviews. Poor, confused

Vincent. He hadn't seemed like a bad guy, really, but I could see how someone might feel smothered under that greedy love. And Jamal's indifferent fling—Sonia might have been hurt, but they were both hurting long before Jamal's gym instructor stepped in.

All of these marriages had failed, I realized, because people had given up on each other. They'd been as good as separated already.

Marcus's words echoed in my ears. *I miss you.*

My participants might have been willing to give up on their marriages, but I wasn't.

At the next intersection, I swung a U-turn, and while I waited for the light to change I typed the new destination into my GPS.

Marcus's pickup game had already started by the time I arrived. He didn't see me at first—he was focused on the game, watching the ball as it passed from player to player, tense and ready, waiting for an opportunity to snap it up and send it arcing over the court.

I settled in at one end of the bleachers and watched the way my husband moved. He could be so intense, and so still, and so watchful. Everything in his posture showed his focus. He was like that in every aspect of his life, wasn't he? He never let his guard down.

Except with me.

Marcus lurched away from his position to steal the ball, then shot down the court, dodging players as he went. At the end of the court he jumped, rising until his fingers could almost brush the hoop, and sent the ball into a slow upward curve so that it came down with a satisfying *swish* into the net.

Marcus turned to high-five his teammates and froze when he saw me on the bench. He flashed me a wide grin before turning back to the game.

Chapter Nineteen

Eliza, Alice, and I waited on the front lawn while Kari packed. The sky above us was remarkably blue. It was one of the last days of true summer, before the leaves began to turn and the breeze became crisp. The sunlight was warm and golden and soft.

Finally, Kari emerged from the house, the baby in one arm, a knapsack of supplies hanging from the other.

"We're not going on vacation," I teased. "It's a walk in the park."

Kari pretended to scowl. "It's not like you don't remember. If it can go wrong and you're not prepared for it, then it will go wrong." She maneuvered Ebrahim into his seat and stuffed the bag in the back. The stroller was one that I'd passed on to her. I didn't envy her the slow, familiar process of bundling the kids into it. Nowadays, all I had to do was shout up the stairs that we were leaving in five, and the kids packed themselves into the car.

"Wanna walk," said Yasmine, reaching for my hand. "Wanna walk with Auntie."

Kari shrugged. "If Auntie doesn't mind."

I took Yasmine's hand and waited while Kari checked over everything. Yasmine tugged at the silver chain around her neck until the dolphin charm I'd given her popped free of her shirt. She jangled the chain so that the dolphin swayed back and forth, and giggled.

We set out at last, with the twins running ahead and Yasmine hurrying to keep pace.

While the kids played on the slides, Kari and I sat on a nearby bench to watch. She told me about the kids and Raife.

"He spoils them so much," she complained. "I have to keep an eye on him to make sure he isn't getting into trouble. Sometimes it's like having three of them."

"A man who spoils his kids," I said with mock gravity. "Is there no greater curse?"

Kari laughed and elbowed me. "Okay, I'll stop babbling. Tell me about school."

"It's good," I said. "I told you about this project, right? We've started interviews."

"Learning anything interesting?" Kari settled Ebrahim on her lap and turned her face toward the sunlight.

"Only that everybody has secrets. Money. Lies. Everybody's hiding something. Pretty much everything commonly forbidden is commonly practiced."

"Any juicy love stories?" Kari asked.

"I wouldn't call them love stories," I said. "But it gives you perspective."

"A grim perspective." Kari leaned over to adjust Ebrahim's blanket. "I don't know how you do it. Doesn't it make you paranoid?"

It had been a few years since Naomi had barged into my kitchen, rattled by her husband's abandonment. You couldn't always see things like that coming. She sure hadn't.

"It gets me thinking," I admitted. "Wondering about everyone. Like . . . like the general. People see the uniform, so they assume he's honorable."

"He's a bad example," Kari insisted. "Besides, everyone knows what he's like. Does it even count as a secret at that point?"

I shrugged.

"I can't imagine living like that," Kari pressed on. "If Raife ever betrayed me?" In this moment, Raife was the one and only man in her world.

"What about you?" I asked. It didn't even occur to Kari that Raife wasn't the only one who could ever look outside their marriage for love.

Kari rolled her eyes. "Yes, it does get hard fighting off the crowds of men that are begging for my sexy post-pregnancy body."

I laughed. "You think they'll mind if you stop for an ice cream on the way home?" I waved to the girls, gesturing that they had five more minutes to play.

Kari groaned. "Twist my arm, huh?"

Part of me wanted to explain to Kari that in matters of the heart, it wasn't about who was good or bad, what was right or wrong, or whether love and desire could be separated from one another—or even if either of those things could exist without the other.

Another part of me wanted to build a fortress around her, to protect her perfect view.

• • • •

We wrapped up our second day of interviews early Friday evening. The participants' stories were starting to run together in my head. Why did it seem like most of the stories had something to do with sex? Affairs. Unrequited love. There was almost always another person involved, if not more than one.

This, I was starting to realize, was common. Uncertainty could kill a marriage.

"Amy!"

I turned to find Sasha waving from the other end of the hall. I stopped and waited for her to catch up.

"You bailed on the last dinner," she said.

I shrugged my embarrassment. "Plans changed. I'm sorry I didn't think to text."

"No problem." Sasha brushed it off with a wave of her hand. "Make it up to me. Come out tonight."

"Let me ask Marcus," I said. I pulled out my phone, then realized the time. He would already be cleaning up from dinner now. He wouldn't mind if I stayed out to get a bite to eat. I texted him to let him know I'd be in late, then dropped my phone into my purse. "I'm coming. Callahan's?"

Sasha nodded, passing me on her way to the door. "I'll see you there. No excuses."

"I'll be there," I said, patting my pockets in search of the keys.

I was glad I'd skipped the last dinner. The game had been fun. At home, Marcus hadn't said anything, but I'd seen the warmth in his eyes, felt his reassurance like a physical touch. He was happy, which made me happy.

Tonight, though, I needed a chance to relax and do something for myself.

• • • •

"Amy, have you met Samuel? He's in his last year of the program." Sasha gestured to the handsome man standing across from her. Samuel flashed me a blinding smile and dipped his head.

"It's a real pleasure to meet you, Amy. Sasha told me about you, but she didn't mention how beautiful you were." His voice was deep, tinged with the hint of a lilting accent. Jamaican, maybe.

Sasha rolled her eyes. "And I mentioned she's married, didn't I?"

"Doesn't make her any less beautiful," said Samuel, sounding wounded. He leaned back against the glossy bar and raised his glass to toast me.

"Ignore him," said Sasha loudly. "He's a shameless flirt, but he's harmless. Thinks he's God's gift to women."

Samuel smiled agreeably, not the least bit offended by Sasha's scorn. "Are you jealous? Don't want me to have eyes for anybody but you, huh?" The sexual tension between them was obvious.

Sasha took my hand. "Come on, there are some other people you should meet."

Not everyone, in fact, was involved in the research project, although I recognized a number of people from campus.

"Tim! 'Vieve!" Sasha waved to two people standing by the far end of the bar, and they made their way toward us.

"You'll like 'Vieve," Sasha whispered. "Tim's pompous, but once you get past that, he's nice enough in his own way."

I let Sasha introduce us, and we threaded our way through the crowd, shaking hands here and there, pausing to gossip about professors and complain about assignments. For the most part, people were friendly, ready to welcome me into the conversation within moments of learning my name.

It was everything The Coffees were supposed to be, but weren't. I found myself laughing with strangers, people who had never been married, and divorcees. A different crowd than the typical military gatherings. No one pretended to follow the unwritten rules of adulthood.

I'd never felt so relaxed at a military function. More than that—I was having fun.

I was laughing at something Tim had said when the hair rose on the back of my neck. I felt as though someone were watching me. I turned my head, scanning the room from the corners of my eyes to see if I was imagining things.

Our mass of graduate students mostly hovered between the bar and the cluster of tables by the door. Across the restaurant, little groups occupied their own spaces. Families, clusters of friends. One long table in the far corner caught my eye, a gathering of mostly men. Sitting at one end of the table, his blue eyes fixed on me, was The Doctor.

I lifted my drink in greeting. He sipped his beer, his mouth forming a smile around the edge of the glass.

"So, what do you think of Samuel?" asked Sasha over my shoulder. I turned my back to him abruptly. I had the irrational fear that Sasha would see the connection between us like a strand of light, obvious and damning.

"He seems nice." I tried to hide my distraction. "Handsome. He likes you."

Even with my back to The Doctor I could feel his gaze.

"I'm thinking I might bring him home tonight," Sasha whispered, squeezing my arm. She stepped away suddenly and changed the topic, and I realized that Samuel had come back toward us.

"Hello again." He slipped his arm around Sasha. "So, Amy, Sasha's been telling me about your project. Is it awkward, talking to men about their ex-wives?"

I tried to come up with a quick answer, but I kept glancing at The Doctor. His presence left me flustered and unable to concentrate.

Samuel raised his eyebrows. "You know, from a married woman's point of view." I realized I hadn't answered at all.

"I guess," I said. It was the best answer I could manage. The drink was going to my head. I finished it off in one gulp and set my empty glass on the bar.

"You need another one, Amy?" asked Sasha.

A peek at The Doctor's table revealed that he'd left. Had he gone home already? I hoped not.

"No, thank you. I'll be right back. Excuse me."

"It's my charm," explained Samuel as I headed off. "Women are often left speechless in my presence."

I made my way toward the back of the pub, relieved to escape the constant buzz of the throng. It was nice to be out, but I'd forgotten how exhausting other people's energy could be.

The restroom was a single, with a brightly lit fixture over the mirror and a little bench across from it. I leaned against the door and closed my eyes for a moment, rubbing my temples. I'd only had one martini and already I was feeling light-headed and too warm. I splashed some cold water on my face and looked up at my reflection.

Someone knocked on the door, and I jumped.

"Just finishing up!" I called, and reached for the handle.

The Doctor stood on the other side, leaning against the wall, waiting for me.

"I was looking for you," he said.

I wasn't sure how to reply, but I couldn't stop the smile that sprang to my lips. We'd never run into each other like this, unexpectedly. His cheeks were flushed, and the longer I looked at him, the brighter his eyes became. He stepped closer.

"I haven't been able to take my eyes off you all night."

I raised my eyebrows. "I noticed."

"You look amazing," he said. He lifted his hand and brushed the hair off my shoulder.

I peered around him to scan the hallway and make sure no one was watching.

"Come here." I pulled him through the door of the women's room. I locked the door behind us, pressed him against the wall, and kissed him.

"Will your friends notice that you're gone?" he asked between kisses.

"Will yours?"

He pulled back for a moment, looking at me in wonder. It seemed I would never get used to his intense gaze. "What is it about you?" he asked. "You can turn me on with one look across the room. How do you do that?" The Doctor's voice was low and husky.

I kissed him again, and his mouth was hungry against mine.

"Amy." He growled my name. "Do you remember what I told you about making promises you don't intend to keep?"

"What am I promising?" I asked, my mouth inches from his.

He placed his hands on my shoulders. "Amy. Look at me."

I did as he asked and we stood there for a moment, breathing hard.

"Come with me to the conference. We'll have time there. I can get away. It won't . . . like this . . ." His words cut off in a groan as my hand explored down his body.

"Stop talking," I whispered. I couldn't answer him in that moment. I wanted him. I needed him. I couldn't wait any longer.

In response, The Doctor put his hands around my waist and pushed me back until I reached the wall, then leaned against me, his hands already roaming across my hem.

His expression was almost feral. "I can't get you out of my head. I think about you all the time."

"What are you thinking?" I reached for his belt, then tugged at the zipper of his khakis.

"About you. Being with you." He fumbled with my skirt, sliding his hands down the back of my panties. "Touching you," he said as his fingers slid into me. "Being inside you." He lifted me up against him. I could feel him hard and hot between my thighs.

I was electric with his voice, his words, his touch. The thrill of him. Before I could say anything more, The Doctor pressed me back against the wall and pushed into me.

I dug my face into his neck to muffle my groan. "You feel so good." I couldn't think about anything but the fullness of him in me, the weight of him against me. I dragged my fingernails across his back and he shuddered. My head buzzed, and I leaned back into him, trying to match his rhythm, gasping his name when I came.

• • • •

Sasha frowned when she saw me. "Where have you been, Amy? I thought you left."

"Bathroom," I said, resisting the urge to check my hair again. "Had to wait. There was someone in there."

If Kari had been there, she would have known. She would have seen in my face that something had changed, would have read my body language and guessed that something was off, even if she would never in a million years have guessed what.

Kari had been my best friend for most of my life. Sasha had known me a few months. She accepted my explanation and turned back toward Samuel, who was stroking her back and telling her something in a soft voice that made her smile widen.

"Amy, can I get you another drink?" asked Tim.

I shook my head. Tim might have been flirting with me, or he might just have been being friendly, but either way I didn't care. My legs were still unsteady beneath me, my heart still pounding, my mouth dry.

"Water," I told the bartender. "Please."

He brought me a glass, and although it was cold I drank it quickly. The coolness cleared my head a little.

"Are you heading out soon?" asked Sasha at my elbow.

I nodded. "Yes. I think so." The Doctor was back at his table, and I couldn't look at him without feeling a mix of affection and guilt and warm arousal. "I should go."

"I'll meet you by the car," said Samuel, pulling out a few bills to pay their tab. I lifted my eyebrows at Sasha, who shrugged unabashedly.

"Single life," she murmured, winking. "I know, it's a bit risqué for you stable married types, but it has its perks."

"I can only imagine," I answered. I even managed to keep my voice expressionless when I said it.

Chapter Twenty

I was sitting in front of my laptop trying to figure out how to summarize our project findings before I had to leave for the kids' activities. I didn't really have time to focus right now, but Professor West wanted everything turned in before next Monday, and I dreaded the idea of having to ask for an extension.

"Conrad!" I called. "Turn off your video game! We're going to be late!"

"I'm coming!" Conrad called. "Five more minutes!"

"We don't have five minutes! Swim practice starts in half an hour!" I called back.

Margie appeared at the top of the stairs. "I'm having trouble with my homework," she said.

I lowered the screen of my computer. "What subject?"

"Math."

"I'll help you," I said. "Bring your book and we can work on it while your brother's at the pool."

Marcus had already told me that it was going to be a long day for him. Hopefully he wouldn't be too much longer. I typed furiously, hoping that my notes would make any kind of sense when I reviewed them later.

Lydia walked in from the kitchen. "Mom? I can't find my felt-tipped markers for drawing class."

"Drawing class?" I asked. That's right, she had drawing tonight, too. I'd completely forgotten. "Don't worry, we'll find them." I saved my work and powered down my laptop.

Eliza and Alice ran to the front door. "Daddy's here!"

"Thank goodness," I muttered, following them.

We met him in the driveway. He didn't get out of the car, just sat there while the girls climbed on him. I filled him in on the situation as quickly as I could.

Marcus nodded. "Tell me what you need me to do. I can drive Conrad if you'll take Lydia."

I ran my hands through my hair, sighing in frustration. "I haven't even started dinner. If we both have to stay during classes . . ."

"If you drop her off, I can pick her up after Conrad's done," Marcus offered.

"I promised Margie I'd help with her homework, too. Maybe if I took her with me and helped her during Lydia's class we could—no, that doesn't solve dinner."

Marcus nodded patiently. "Should I pick up something to eat on the way home?"

Lydia poked her head out the front door. "Mom, I still can't find my markers. You said you'd help me look."

"Right, I'm coming. Has Conrad come down yet?" I headed back inside to track down my son.

He wasn't in the living room. I looked up at the clock and groaned.

"Conrad, if you're not down here in fifteen seconds . . . ," I began.

"Okay, Mom! I'm almost ready!"

Margie still hovered at the top of the stairs, almost forgotten in the hubbub, still clinging to her math assignment.

I looked back outside to find the twins bouncing on Marcus's lap, pretending to drive the car. All the clubs, all the classes, all of our interests and hobbies—sometimes it felt like a juggling act. What was the point of all this mayhem when, at the end of the night, it was just going to leave us frustrated and irritable?

"Amy?" called Marcus, noting my expression. "Are you okay?"

"I will be," I called back. "When the three of you come home with pizza."

He gestured toward the house. "No swim practice? No art class?"

"There's been a change of plans."

A smile spread over Marcus's face. "Sounds like a *better* plan." Within two minutes, he had the twins buckled in and was backing the car out of the driveway. That solved, I headed back inside and up the stairs.

Conrad finally emerged from his room, wearing his swim trunks and a T-shirt, a towel thrown over his shoulder. He looked up at me sheepishly.

"You," I pointed to Conrad, "are going to go help Margie finish her homework. Next time, be ready or the wagon train leaves without you."

"Okay," said Conrad. "Yes, ma'am."

Lydia and I searched the house and finally found her markers jammed into the bottom of her book bag.

"At least you'll have them for next week," I told her. "This time, put them somewhere you won't lose them."

Within half an hour Marcus had returned with dinner, and my whole family was piled on the couch, steaming pizza boxes open on the coffee table, laughing at the TV. They'd decided on a silly movie, featuring talking dogs and a predictable plot, but I was leaning against Marcus and my children were chuckling at all the stupid lines. I finally began to unwind.

"We should do this more often," Marcus whispered in my ear.

In my pocket, my phone buzzed with a message. "Probably Sasha checking to see how much I've gotten done," I said, and ignored it.

"Are you going to get behind tonight?" asked Marcus.

"Worth it," I assured him. "I'll find time to catch up."

"I'm thinking of taking the kids to see my parents this weekend," he said. "They've been asking when we'll visit, and this way you'll have some peace and quiet to get your work done."

I sighed and nestled in closer to his embrace. "You are the best husband I could possibly imagine. I love you so much."

He kissed my temple. "I love you too."

When the film ended, we told the kids to get ready for bed. Then, one by one, we tucked them in and made them promise to have their lights out within a half hour.

None of this was particularly glamorous, but it was my life. My family. Just having us together in one room made me happy; having us all asleep under the same roof made me feel safe.

In our room, I emptied my pockets, ready to climb into bed. I'd almost forgotten about the text message, but when I pulled out my phone, there it was.

Not from Sasha, but from The Doctor. One line. *The conference—will you come?*

• • • •

Saturday morning, in a silent house, I sat down with the project findings. With no kids in the house there were no distractions, and no excuses for putting off my work. I made myself some coffee and curled into a ball on one corner of the couch.

Most participants, I typed, *seemed to feel that their lives were stuck. They were trapped in holding patterns, living for other people as much as for themselves.*

I paused, my fingers hovering over the keyboard. Sasha would say that this was the problem with marriage. That when you swore vows to someone, you started to make compromises, and in the end neither of you got the life you really wanted.

But that wasn't true for me. I loved Marcus. I loved the kids. I hadn't settled—I'd discovered a kind of happiness that would never have occurred to the carefree, wild-child teenager I used to be. I'd given my heart to Marcus.

Sasha's theory on commitment was to love the person, not the relationship. That brought to mind what Charles had said. Something about how people agreed to be right for each other. What if loving two people felt right to you?

Love. That was a powerful word. A word tangled up with expectations, and often confused with judgment.

A large portion of the participants seemed to feel that the quality of their lives had not improved significantly by having an affair. Those who ended up with a new partner often felt that their new partner was a better match, but those involved in flings, rather than relationships based on mutual compatibility, frequently ended up alone, and usually did not feel that their affairs had led to an improved quality of life. Participants whose affairs had been purely physical in nature tended to fall into the latter category.

Maybe I was just stating the obvious. Kari would think so. An affair was a broken promise, severing the trust between two people indefinitely. That was her theory. If Raife ever fell for another woman, she'd either blame him for betraying her, or herself for failing to keep him. But was there ever only one person to blame? Sometimes there's a victim of the affair, and sometimes an affair is committed by the victim of a marriage.

Did it have to mean the end of the relationship? What if someone needed the relationship to become a better person? What if the relationship gave them something that made their marriage stronger? Had the person hurt their marriage, or helped it?

Participants whose affairs were based primarily on escapism, rather than self-discovery or love, often ended up as lonely and confused as their abandoned partners.

I'd never asked Naomi why Rob left. It hadn't seemed important at the time. I'd assumed that he'd found someone younger or gotten bored with their marriage. Maybe I'd been wrong. Maybe he'd met someone amazing, who opened his heart more than Naomi ever could have. Maybe she'd had an affair and he'd found out. Maybe their marriage had been as good as over long before they split.

Why was I so used to assuming that relationships were simple: all or nothing? I should have known by now that they are complex, bound or broken for reasons that observers may never understand.

Of the participants who felt that their affairs had led to personal growth, the majority were those whose marriages were not the source of their unhappiness. This group was made up of people who felt that their personalities, and not their existing relationships, were ill-suited to the expectations of the people around them.

My relationship with The Doctor had nothing to do with Marcus. He would never be able to see it that way, but it was the truth. I didn't want to replace him.

Corrina always told me that I didn't need to depend on another person for my happiness.

When The Doctor was in my life, I felt better. The two parts of me that had always felt mutually exclusive could exist together.

Do something for yourself, Corrina had told me.

I reached for my phone and texted The Doctor the word I'd been fighting all week.

Yes.

• • • •

The conference had taken over most of a hotel, with three or four simultaneous presentations scheduled throughout the complex. I had assumed that there would be a few hundred attendees, but I soon realized that there must be closer to several thousand.

A gangly student in skinny jeans and a blue polo lounged at the information desk.

"Excuse me?" I said. "Do you have a schedule or something?"

He flashed me a brilliant smile and dug out a fistful of papers. "Schedule, map, lecture guide, vendor listings . . ."

"I'm only here for one lecture," I said.

He shrugged. "Take them. You should check out the rest of the conference if you get a chance. There's a lot going on."

I leafed through the papers until I found The Doctor's name, then checked the clock. I had another half hour until his presentation started. I might as well look around.

Besides, the idea of running into The Doctor before his lecture left me a little fluttery.

There were dozens of booths advertising pharmaceuticals, new research findings, surgical centers, coalitions, and other conferences. Most of the booths were aimed at professionals.

As I wandered among the displays, it occurred to me that I had never been so close to The Doctor's world. I'd seen him in the hospital or met up with him in person, but we'd lived in our own private world, except when our circles overlapped as they had in Callahan's.

When he'd invited me to the conference then, he'd invited me into his space.

And I had come willingly.

• • • •

By the time I arrived, the room was almost full. I found a seat in the back, away from the rest of the crowd. I knew it was unlikely that The Doctor would be able to spot me in the audience, but I liked the thought of him looking for me.

The Doctor took the stage, and the room fell silent. He was dressed in his Army Service Uniform, clean-cut, and as always his presence demanded immediate attention. When the moderator introduced him, she listed a few of the awards that The Doctor had received, mostly for articles he'd published on weight-loss surgery.

He spoke passionately of his experiences from his many years in the field of military medicine. Parts of the lecture surrounding nutritional health were familiar. It was similar, I realized, to the one he'd given patients in the hospital shortly after we met. Back then he'd kept things simple, but here, surrounded by his peers, he spoke with more enthusiasm, moving his hands for emphasis as he warmed to his theme.

The first time I'd seen him present in public, I'd finally admitted to myself that I was attracted to him.

This time, watching his face light up as he spoke and the lines around his eyes disappear, seeing him as genuinely proud and easy and self-assured as I'd ever seen him, I finally admitted something else.

I was in love with The Doctor.

Chapter Twenty-One

After The Doctor's presentation ended, a row of conference attendees lined up to ask him questions and thank him for his time. I hung back, listening vaguely to the questions, focusing mostly on The Doctor's expression as he answered.

One by one, the others left, and only when the last woman thanked him and shook his hand did I get up from my chair.

"I saw you from across the room," The Doctor said when I reached him. He folded his arms and smiled down at me, his weight resting on one leg, his mouth quirked up in a small smile. "I'm glad you decided to come."

I smiled back at him. "Me too. What do you have next?"

The Doctor looked around at the empty conference room. "Well, let me think, there's a Q-and-A on program implementation, and I think the keynote speaker starts in about an hour . . ."

"So you're busy," I said. "If I've caught you at a bad time, I'm sorry. It's just that I have this, well, this condition, and I was hoping you could help me with it."

The Doctor raised his eyebrows. "Depending on the nature of your emergency, I can clear my schedule."

"I would so appreciate that," I said, reaching out to touch his arm. "You wouldn't know how much."

He looked down at where my hand rested on his sleeve. At that moment, I didn't care if anyone saw us. Frankly, I didn't care what one person at this conference thought. I turned that revelation over and over in my mind—*I love him*—and tried to convey it to him with this one simple touch.

The Doctor's eyes were bright when he looked up at me. "Well. Let's get that looked at."

He led me toward the elevators, and we kept our distance, as if we were two strangers talking.

"Can you tell me your symptoms?" he asked in a low voice.

"Elevated blood pressure. High temperature."

"Strange," he said seriously, although he couldn't keep the smile off his lips. "I've been experiencing similar symptoms. Also shortness of breath."

"Yes," I said earnestly. "And I'm getting this strange feeling in my chest, like . . ."

"Cardiac event," interrupted The Doctor. "Very serious. You were right to call me in."

We reached the elevators. There were a few groups of people, many of them wearing conference badges. We avoided them and joined a larger family instead. The Doctor stood against the mirrored wall and I stood with my back against him, making space for the family. He put his hands on my waist to pull me closer. The children jostled each other as the doors closed.

"Sorry," said their red-eyed mother. "We've been stuck on a plane all day."

"That doesn't sound like much fun," said The Doctor, massaging my shoulders. It would have looked like a casual caress to any observer, but I was increasingly aware of every point of contact between us.

We left them on the fifth floor while they continued up. The Doctor took my hand on our way down the hall. I tried to calm my breathing as we walked, but just thinking about our last encounter in Callahan's made my skin prickle with heat. He didn't let go until we'd reached his room and he had to rifle through his pockets for the room key.

It was an anonymous, spartan room, and like any hotel room it was dominated by the bed.

The Doctor pulled off his badge, folded the lanyard, and lay it on the bedside table. Then he turned to me, and I felt all the blood rush to my face. I'd never seen him look so tender, so open.

I started to say his name, but he lifted a hand to my cheek, running his thumb across the corner of my mouth, his blue eyes scanning my face.

Did he have any idea how much I wanted him?

He stepped closer, kissing me deep and slow. We'd never been alone like this, never had a chance to take our time like this.

When we broke apart, he was breathing hard.

"So," he murmured, "you'd mentioned chest pains?" One hand fell to my left breast, and my pulse quickened beneath his fingers. He smiled at my expression. "Ah. And there's the elevated heart rate you mentioned." He bent down, pressing his lips to my throat.

I leaned into his touch. I wasn't ready to join in with his teasing. I didn't want to talk, didn't want to think. I only wanted to feel him.

Every time before, I could have been anyone. I knew how I felt about him, and I suspected that he felt the same way, but I'd always wondered if I could have been any pretty patient who needed his help. If he'd have told anyone he looked twice at, *You're in the ninety-fifth percentile of women.* If I was somehow falling short by not earning the highest rank of all.

This time, though, was different. He'd invited me in. Into his life, into his heart. And now, with his slow-burning touch, I could feel the shape of the thing between us for the first time.

It wasn't just desire. It was need. He needed something from me, and I needed something from him, and what we had to offer each other wasn't a feeling that could be provided by any stolen touch, any soft caress, any kiss. I cared about the man inside his body. If physicality was the best way to express that caring, then I would yield to it every time.

When he pulled me down to the bed, I went willingly. He undressed me slowly, giving his fingers a chance to explore every inch of me, his eyes following.

It was one thing to grab hold of someone, have them, and send them on their way. When his mouth grazed my nipples or trailed down across my belly button to the wet warmth between my legs, he wasn't taking something from me. We were sharing something. That, as much as anything, was why I cried out when he teased me with his tongue, sliding two fingers inside me.

"Amy," he said afterward, but that was all.

It was my turn to push him down beneath me, undoing his shirt one button at a time, sliding my hands across his hips and thighs until I reached his belt and unbuckled it. My turn to lay him bare before me, then explore him with my tongue until he pushed me away.

"Please," he said softly, and I slid him inside me.

There was urgency, too, as there had always been between us. A fierce wanting, a reckless give-and-take. But this time we were slow, gradual, so that the climax, when it came, left us both breathless and satisfied.

• • • •

We dozed awhile, drunk on our lovemaking. When The Doctor finally rolled toward me, propping his head up on his elbow, his eyes were still heavy-lidded with desire.

"I don't know if this is terribly unsexy, but I'm starving."

"Give me a minute to regain feeling in my limbs," I said. "I'm not sure I can walk at the moment."

He kissed my cheek, then got to his feet. "We should go out for dinner," he said. "There are plenty of options around here. How do you feel about Chinese?"

Chinese food reminded me of a family ritual I didn't want to think about. "I need to get my strength back. Better make it a steak."

"Protein. Just what I would have prescribed." He walked to the bathroom, and I watched him go, appreciating the view.

On our way out of the hotel, I put my arm through his. He stopped at the reception desk and asked for restaurant suggestions. The clerk gave us directions, not so much as batting an eye at my presence. For all he knew, I belonged there.

We walked the three blocks to the restaurant, chatting easily as we went. The place turned out to be a hole-in-the-wall Italian restaurant, and by the smell from the sidewalk, the clerk had good taste.

The Doctor ordered a beer with his dinner. I decided on white wine.

"So," said The Doctor, "are you heading home tonight?" He spun his fork on the table, not meeting my eyes.

I shook my head.

He looked up at me in surprise. "Can you? I mean, that's . . . Amy . . ."

"I'll have to leave early in the morning, but yes, I can stay."

The whole time we ate he kept looking up at me, a little smile tugging at the corner of his mouth. When the waiter offered to refill my glass, I declined. I didn't need the alcohol to feel giddy and light.

• • • •

That night, in the hotel room, The Doctor slid beneath the sheets first. He lay down and opened his arms, waiting for me to join him. I curled into the curve of his side, my knees brushing his, our feet touching. I tried to calm my breathing, to slow it as I would if I were sleeping, but I didn't feel tired.

"I have a call-back interview next week," The Doctor said into the silence. "I'm hoping this one works out. Only two more months until I go on terminal leave."

"Ah, retirement, when you can finally grow out your beard," I teased. I was so used to seeing him in uniform—it was hard to imagine him moving on. "Be patient. The right job will present itself."

"Yeah. But it would be nice to have something lined up before retirement rolls around." He tilted his head toward mine until his chin rested on my hair. After a little while he added, "I've thought about this for months. I don't mean here, just . . . you. With me. With all the time we want."

I nodded, my cheek pressed against his chest. "I have too."

"I always feel good when I'm with you."

My imagination hadn't been perfect. I'd imagined the warmth of him, the feel of his body against mine, the stillness, the peace of near-sleep. I sighed and settled closer. This was exactly what I'd pictured.

"I feel a lot of things with you," I said as I ran my fingertips across his belly.

"Amy." The Doctor shifted, rolling on to his side so that I lay next to him. I could barely make out the silhouette of his face in the darkness. Only his eyes, two bright points in the dim room. "I love everything about you."

I shifted my weight and rolled onto him, leaning down to kiss him with my hands pressed against his shoulders. "It's a mutual feeling," I assured him.

But.

I hadn't imagined the uneasiness. The way my heart was pulled in two directions at once: toward The Doctor, and away from him. I knew that there were people who could love more than one person at a time, and I'd never really understood them. How could anyone have enough love to give two people at once? How could they fall in love with someone when they were already deeply in love with someone else? I understood now. I was one of those people. I felt like a wishbone, pulled by two separate men. I would break, and only one of them would get what they wanted.

Unless I chose first.

He pulled me back down toward him. "I want you."

"I'm right here," I said.

• • • •

I woke when it was still dark, and I could not go back to sleep. Beside me, The Doctor was snoring very softly, one arm draped across my body. His breath ruffled my hair.

I had not woken up to anyone but my husband since I was in my twenties. I was used to sleeping beside Marcus in our bed.

Until now, I'd been able to compartmentalize things. When I was with The Doctor, I thought about The Doctor. When I was with Marcus, I thought about Marcus. My feelings for one didn't diminish my feelings for the other.

I shifted so that I could examine The Doctor's sleeping form. He looked almost like a different person when he was asleep, and in the hazy dawn light I was able to make out things I'd never noticed about him before. He had a spattering of freckles across his collarbone. There was a white scar on one shoulder, so smooth that it was barely noticeable.

I reached out to trace my finger along the scar.

At my touch, The Doctor woke, blinking at me. "What time is it?"

I rolled to look at the digital clock on the nightstand. "Almost five thirty."

"Still early." He rolled closer and gave me a delicious smile. "Good. I'm not ready to get out of bed just yet." His hands began to roam my body.

As we held each other close and began to kiss, gently at first and then in earnest, I felt a bittersweet ache in my chest.

This, I decided, would be the last time I would make love to him. It had to be. Things were already drifting beyond my control.

I held him tighter. I didn't want it to end. When it did, the pleasure he gave me was tempered with regret. I wanted just a little longer with him. Just another day.

I was always going to want another day. I felt as if I were standing before a very thin line, sticking my toes out over the edge.

"Let's stay in bed all day," said The Doctor. My head rested against his chest, and I could hear the pounding of his heart beneath me.

Reluctantly, I shook my head. "I should get going."

"Stay for breakfast," The Doctor suggested.

It could be like dinner last night, my heart said. *Just the two of you, eating, laughing.* But every moment I stayed felt like a promise, and every promise I made The Doctor was a promise to Marcus I'd broken.

"I can't go down to the conference in the same clothes I wore last night. How would that look?" I hadn't brought spare clothes. I hadn't planned on staying. I began to loosen my legs from his, but he tightened his hold on me.

"I suppose it would look like you had a good night."

I laughed and wriggled free of his grip. "Better than good." I sat up and began the search for my scattered clothes.

The Doctor caught my wrist and looked up at me, mouth slightly open, in hopeful anticipation of a kiss. I obliged, and we lingered, his hands tangling in my hair.

He pulled me back down against him. "Stay," he said again.

My resolve wavered. I would love to spend the day in bed with him, kissing him, making love to him. I wanted him. I loved him.

The trouble, of course, was that I already wanted someone else. The Doctor looked after me as attentively as Marcus ever had, but it was Marcus I couldn't imagine a life without.

I leaned my forehead against his and shook my head.

We kissed once more, and then I rose and dressed slowly. I could feel his eyes on me as I pulled my clothes on. When I was ready, he pulled a sheet free from the tangled bedding and wrapped it around himself to walk me to the door.

I stopped and slid my arms around his waist, pulling him close, pressing my face into his bare chest.

"I don't know how I'm going to focus today," he murmured.

"Good thing your presentation was yesterday, then."

He puffed a laugh. "Indeed. Amy, I'm glad you came. This was . . ."

I nodded. "I'm glad too."

At last we let go, and I smoothed my hair, and he kissed my cheek, and we squeezed our hands together before he opened the door and I stepped out.

I waved.

He waved.

And neither of us said good-bye before the door swung shut between us.

• • • •

On the walk down the hallway, then in the elevator on my way to the parking level, I kept my eyes on the floor. I didn't want anyone to see what I was feeling.

Part of me wished that The Doctor would chase after me, beg me to stay, seduce me again.

"Keep going, Amy," I muttered to myself, and dug through my purse in search of my keys.

In the car, my hands shook on the steering wheel. I was breathing hard, trying to keep back the tears.

I could turn the car back off, go back to the room, stay for breakfast, stay for lunch, sneak home just in time to convince my family I'd been there all weekend. But then I would be sneaking forever, and I would tear myself in two between what Marcus wanted and what The Doctor wanted.

If I turned around, that would be a choice. If I started driving, that would be a choice too, and one way or the other I would have to live with the consequences.

Not just today. Not just tomorrow. Every day.

I took another deep breath, but the tears came anyway.

• • • •

At home, I stripped off my clothes.

I ran a hot shower, washing The Doctor's scent out of my hair, steaming his caress out of my skin. I wished I could erase the image of him from my mind as easily.

I made a pot of coffee and sat down with my laptop. My notes were almost finished, and I wanted to have everything sent before my family came home. I didn't want time to think. I didn't want time to question myself.

I opened the computer to add one last line. *Love is part of every human's experience, by chance or by coincidence. When it thrives, it brings us joy and fulfillment. When it fades—or, worse yet, when we surrender it—love lays us open to the deepest pain, to lingering regrets, to self-doubt. Can we believe in the sensation of love even when we can't find a way to nurture it? To sustain it?*

I rubbed at my eyes with the back of my hand.

Yes, we can. We must. Love is the emotion that gives everything else in our lives meaning.

I was adding the attachment when I heard the rumble of the engine in the driveway, then the clamor of voices.

Any minute my family would come in, bubbling over with news about their trip and too much pent-up energy from the long drive. They'd want all my attention and all my love, and they'd have it.

They'd always have it.

I typed the signature of my email. Then, as they opened the front door, I hit *Send.*

Chapter Twenty-Two

At Kari's insistence, I agreed to attend the Thanksgiving Coffee. She didn't have to work hard to persuade me. I needed the distraction.

My last visit to The Coffee felt like it had taken place a lifetime ago. In the time since I'd moved here from O'ahu, it felt like little had changed. I was surrounded by the same faces, the same smiles, the same conversations. I found a chair in the center of the living room that allowed me to see most of the surrounding rooms and the guests within. I purposely placed myself near a small group of women deep in conversation. I sat close enough that I didn't appear isolated, but far enough away that I wasn't expected to participate in their conversation. I wanted to listen, but I didn't feel that I had much to say.

I reached for my phone for what felt like the millionth time, then set it down without even powering the screen on. What was the point? I was waiting for a message to which I wouldn't even let myself reply.

I just wanted to know that The Doctor was thinking about me as much as I thought about him.

"Amy?" said a woman. I looked up in surprise to find the general's wife standing there, then rose to hug her in greeting. She had on her perfect smile, but appeared more relaxed than I remembered. I'd always thought of her as a bit snooty, but now I felt uncharitable.

"We haven't seen you in quite some time," she said.

I smiled. "Oh, well, you know, with Marcus's deployment and the kids and my program, I'm afraid I haven't been able to attend as often."

As we spoke, the general walked by and shook the hands of a few women. I could see that his wife was distracted by him, and she narrowed her eyes slightly at her husband. I felt for her. Did she always have to keep an eye on him, wondering who he'd flirt with next? Did she know he'd made a pass at me at one of my first Coffees in the area?

She turned her attention back to me. "If you ever need anything, just call me. You know I'm here to help."

"Thank you," I said, surprised. There was no doubt in my mind that if I called her, she would offer whatever help she could give. I was equally clear that I would never call.

We said our good-byes, and I returned to my seat. The general's wife drifted off to join her husband, greeting the other women. She knew his ways. Most likely the other women were whispering about her husband behind her back. Still, she'd made her choice, and she was standing by him.

We all made our choices.

I decided to hunt down Kari, and found her in the kitchen with a small knot of women, most of whom I recognized.

Kari had found a way to be part of this group, had even made a few good friends here. I was glad that made her happy.

I walked over and stood with the group, trying to catch up on their conversation. All I could think about was whether I should check my phone. I wanted to hear from The Doctor—no, what I really wanted was to see him, to hold him, to kiss him. I wanted to ask him questions. Was he thinking about me? Had he, too, fallen in love? Did he, too, know it was over?

All of this made me even sadder, because I knew the answer to every question was yes.

"Are you okay?" Kari whispered.

I nodded, jolting back to the real world. "Sorry, I was thinking about something."

With a last worried glance, Kari let it slide. She turned back to the group. I stepped in close and tried to focus on joining in.

Cheryl, a plump blonde I remembered dimly from earlier Coffees, was talking about her family. "I've been going to yoga for a few weeks. Joe thinks it's a waste of time, but it's helping me relax. The kids are both on the honor roll this year. They just took tests in their age brackets, and let me tell you, all our hard work is really paying off . . ."

As the conversation continued, I looked back and forth between the women, smiling and nodding to show that I was paying attention. I listened for a while, trying to think of something to add, but I couldn't think of one thing to say that these women would find interesting. The other women took turns bragging about their children's achievements, their husbands' jobs and promotions. Their lives didn't sound so different than mine.

Except that these women didn't seem to speak much about themselves, but lit up from within while speaking about their husbands. Were any of these women really content, or were they like the people I'd spoken to during the interviews? Maybe everyone had a weight dragging at their heart, just like I did. A secret they would never share with anyone.

What was The Doctor thinking about right now?

I slowly turned and stepped away from the little cluster of women. I could really use some wine. Anything to get him off my mind.

"Hey." Kari caught up with me and spoke in a whisper. "Ames? You okay?"

I smiled at her, although the expression felt wooden and unconvincing on my face. "Yes, sorry, I've just got a lot on my mind."

Kari frowned. "It looked like more than just a moment of spacing."

"It's really nothing," I said.

Kari examined me again, then looped her arm through mine. She led me toward the door, practically dragging me along. We smiled politely and said our good-byes on the way out.

Honestly, I didn't mind having an excuse to leave. Even on a good day The Coffee was tedious. Today it had been overwhelming.

Kari slipped into my car, the black two-seater Marcus had gotten me for my birthday. "Thanks for coming with me. It's a lot more fun with you here. Do you think you'll start coming regularly again?" She sounded hopeful.

"Maybe." I shrugged. "I don't really know anyone. Or fit in, for that matter."

"You just have to give people a chance. Get to know them, and let them get to know you."

"I'll keep that in mind," I said as I started the car.

Kari put her hand on mine to stop me. "Ames?" she said softly. "Something's wrong. You seem . . . I don't know. Off. Tired."

"School's taking a lot out of me," I hedged.

She kept looking at me, and I squirmed under her gaze. Kari knew that I was holding back, but I wasn't ready to discuss The Doctor with her.

I had a sudden memory of his face, his deep blue eyes.

I really didn't want to think about him.

"There," she said, "just now, you looked, I don't know. Happy and then sad again."

"It's nothing," I assured her.

She didn't let go. "Is it Marcus?"

"No," I said, taken aback. "Of course not. Marcus is great." I paused. "I haven't felt like myself lately. I'm just trying to find the balance between what I'm supposed to do and what I want to do." I never lied to Kari, but I didn't know how to explain that I'd been feeling more like myself than ever, and that was part of what was hurting me.

"Is there anything I can do to help? You know I'm here for you."

I leaned back in my seat and put a hand on her arm. "Kari, you know I would come to you first if I needed a friend, right?"

"I would hope so," she said solemnly.

"I would."

Kari held out her hand, pinkie finger extended. "Promise me."

I gaped at her. "Are you serious?"

"Pinkie promise me that you'll tell me what's really going on when you're ready to talk about it."

I offered my pinkie, and she clenched it in hers.

"Ice cream?" she asked.

I grinned. "I'm already on my way."

It was comforting to know that I'd have a support network if I needed one. Lonely, too, to know that no matter how bad it got, I would probably never be ready to tell Kari the whole truth.

We sat next to each other in a booth at the ice cream parlor and talked for a long time, mostly about our families. I didn't realize that she'd completely taken my mind off The Doctor until my phone buzzed. I checked it discreetly, telling myself that it wouldn't be him, then cursed my heart for pounding when I realized that it was.

When can I see you? was all it said.

I wished he'd said more. I wished he'd said nothing at all. I shoved my phone back into my purse and promised myself I wouldn't reply.

• • • •

"When is your mother getting in?" Marcus asked.

"Wednesday morning. Did you talk to your parents yet?"

"They're staying home," he said. "My brothers will be there."

"I'm sorry we don't get to see them much." I poked through the cupboards, making sure I had everything on my shopping list. "Could they all have come here?"

"I mentioned that to them, but I have to say, a quiet holiday sounds pretty much ideal." Marcus abandoned the dishes and came over and put his arms around me. "And you're worn out from that project, I know."

The project was long since over, but I didn't correct him. After all, it was the endings of things that had made me so tired lately.

• • • •

Classes stopped on Tuesday, with the rest of the week off for the holiday. Sasha and I met for a drink on Tuesday night to celebrate the long vacation.

Callahan's was as polished and sultry as ever, but I wasn't really in the mood for it. The low jazz in the background sounded melancholy rather than soothing.

"I sort of miss doing interviews," said Sasha, swirling her gin and tonic. "People's personal lives are so interesting."

I leaned forward on the bar, turning my back to the bathrooms. "Speaking of personal lives, how's Samuel?" It was hard to keep myself from watching the door every time it opened. The thought of The Doctor appearing again at the back table excited me and scared me at the same time.

Sasha rolled her eyes and shrugged. "He's getting a bit clingy. I think I might cut him loose."

"Is that how it works?" I asked. "You keep everyone at arm's length to keep them from working their way into your heart?"

"Now you sound like him. He says it's selfish of me not to allow him into my life." She leaned her chin in her palm, looking thoughtfully up at the glasses hanging over the bar. "But I think he assumes that loving him is a selfless act."

"So you never fantasize about making a life with someone?" I glanced back at the bathroom before I could stop myself. I remembered the warmth of The Doctor's lips on mine, and it thrilled me.

She wrinkled her nose. "I have. But the prospect of building a life with someone . . . I don't know. A husband. Kids. Putting all these other people before myself. Honestly? It scares me."

Did she have it right? If you didn't fall in love, did that protect your heart from being broken?

"Maybe you'll meet someone who convinces you the fear is worth it."

"Amy." Sasha sat up, and her casual attitude returned. "Do you really believe that two people can be everything to each other? That there is one person waiting for me? One person for life is simply not natural. And it's no fun."

I felt bad for Sasha that she feared love. If only she knew what love could feel like. How Marcus loved me. How The Doctor loved me. If she knew how that felt, she wouldn't fear the unknown that came along with it.

"It's possible that there's more than one, you know. *The One.*" I made air quotes for emphasis. "But I think the secret is that you have to love someone as if they *are* The One and expect the same in return. When you both do that, it can work."

"You mean compromise with someone in order to live an imperfect life?" She laughed. "The thought of staying in one place and living a life filled with responsibilities, and never being allowed to fall in love again . . . it doesn't seem worth it." She tossed back the rest of her drink. "Anyway, the selection of men in this city is too plentiful. How can I choose just one?"

I laughed. "All right, all right."

"Do you want another?" she asked, signaling the bartender.

I swirled my glass so that the ice rattled in my mostly full cup. "I think I'm done, actually. I'm feeling a little under the weather."

"Oh, too bad," said Sasha. "I hope it's nothing serious."

Nothing more serious than a broken heart, I almost said, but Sasha wasn't the person to open up to. We never spoke that seriously, or that intimately. She might understand my choices more than most, but she'd view my heartbreak as something I'd brought on myself. Part of me was thinking the same thing.

"I'll be fine." I hugged her good-bye. "And try to be nice to Samuel."

"I'll think about it," she said. "Happy Thanksgiving."

On my way out, I stopped by the bathroom. I locked the door behind me and leaned against the wall, thinking about The Doctor. He'd taken such good care of me. He'd awakened a part of me that I forgot was there and made me feel alive.

Then I thought about Marcus. He was the only person that I could imagine creating a family with. Marcus loved me unconditionally. He took care of me and protected our family with everything he had in him.

I was so fortunate to have loved them both, and I was a better person for having known them.

No matter how I was feeling at the moment, I wouldn't change a thing.

• • • •

Corrina flew in Wednesday. Our only other Thanksgiving guests were Kari and her family. They'd agreed to bring mashed potatoes and rolls, which left us with most of the other cooking.

Marcus was in a playful mood. He and Lydia made up a song to sing to the turkey while it cooked, and he made so many puns about gravy, stuffing, and the Mayflower that even Conrad laughed.

Sitting at a table with all these people who were so dear to me, I felt at peace for the first time in weeks.

Kari pushed her plate aside and rubbed her belly, catching my eye. "Thanksgiving tradition," she said. "What are you grateful for?"

The kids groaned.

Kari shook her head. "What, it's so hard to name one thing? I'm thankful for my good friends and my wonderful family. There, that's two."

"Cheers to that!" Corrina raised her wine glass to Kari's. "To friends and family. And Paris," she added.

Marcus squeezed my hand. "I'm thankful to be home this year," he said. I smiled at him and squeezed back.

Raife lifted his half-empty beer in agreement. "Amen."

The kids began a halfhearted recitation of what they were thankful for, and Marcus leaned closer to whisper in my ear. "I'm grateful for everything. For you. For our beautiful family. For our life together."

I clung to Marcus's hand and nodded, blinking rapidly to disguise my watery eyes. When my turn came around, I said, "I'm grateful for love."

And it was true. Love had meant a lot of heartache lately. Still, in that company, it was easy to see that the good things love had brought into my life far outweighed the bad.

• • • •

Kari, Raife, and Marcus shepherded the kids into the backyard after dinner while Corrina and I cleared the table. I was running the hot water when my phone buzzed in my pocket. I glanced down at the message, then reread it once. Twice. A third time.

I'll always be glad that we met. You're forever in my heart. I didn't have to look to see who it was from.

My peaceful feeling from dinner evaporated, and I choked back a sob. The pain of losing The Doctor hit me again, as though something had physically struck me. The worst part was that I could make this pain stop if I just called him, told him to meet me somewhere, if I just gave in.

Corrina stepped into the room, carrying a gravy boat and fistful of silverware. Her eyebrows rose when she saw my face.

"Amy?" she asked.

"I'm fine," I said. "I'm fine." The tears were already spilling down my cheeks.

She set everything in the sink and took my hand, leading me to a chair. "Okay, honey, what's wrong?"

I sat reluctantly. "I'm fine," I repeated. Obviously I was not.

"Let me look at you," she said, taking both my hands in hers. "Why do you always feel like you have to be fine? You're allowed to have other feelings, you know."

"I'll be okay. It's just that so much has changed." I wiped at my face with my sleeve. "I've changed."

"I could see that the moment I got here." Corrina leaned over to brush away the last of my tears. "It's in your aura. It's not a bad thing, either."

"I know." I lay my hands flat on the table and took a deep breath to steady myself. "I'll find a way to put it all back together."

"Oh, Amy." Corrina shook her head. "If only all things were that easy. One of the hardest lessons I've had to learn is that I can't fix everything. Not all things can be mended. Not all things *should* be mended. Sometimes leaving things alone is the best way to handle them."

I looked up at her and met her eyes for the first time since she'd arrived. Her eyebrows were crinkled together, and she was frowning. When I was a girl, I'd thought her childish. When I was a new mother, I'd thought her selfish. Now, I could see that she was just like everyone else, living her life in the best way she knew how.

"You're always telling me to be happy."

"You misunderstood, darling. I'm not telling you that you have to *fake* being happy. I'm telling you to do whatever you have to do to *make* yourself happy."

"I'm trying," I told her.

"Well, if you want my opinion, you're doing a wonderful job in this life. It's a pleasure to watch you come into your own." She smiled wryly. "And I don't think you need your mother telling you what to do."

She didn't sound bitter, just matter-of-fact.

"Thanks." I got up and kissed her cheek. "I'm glad to have you here, Mom."

When she stepped back out into the dining room, I pulled out my phone again.

I'll be thinking of you, I typed. *Always.*

Chapter Twenty-Three

"Three weeks until graduation," said Sasha, slipping off her sandals. "Can you believe it?"

I smiled up into the sunlight. "Not really. It went by so fast."

"I hear Nurul's top in our class," said Sasha. "She already has three job offers lined up. Do you ever feel a little behind the curve? She's young enough to be our illegitimate daughter."

I snorted behind my hand. "Speak for yourself. Maybe *you're* old enough to be her mother."

"You've got me there. And we're not doing too badly for ourselves." Sasha dug her toes into the campus lawn. "I've gotten a few offers too, actually."

I raised my eyebrows at her in surprise. "Really? Where?"

"You don't need to sound so surprised." She closed her eyes and took a deep breath. "One here and another in California."

"Oh." I folded my arms and rested them on my knees. "Which one are you going to take?"

"I don't know yet. Why? Would you miss me if I moved out West?"

I pulled up a few blades of grass, crushing them until they turned my fingertips green. "We'd keep in touch."

"Of course," said Sasha, as if this were obvious.

I tilted my head to examine her. She looked so carefree, as she always did. I wasn't sure I believed her. If she moved away, she'd have no reason to visit. She'd probably drift away into her new life and out of mine.

Which was okay, I decided. It wouldn't mean that our friendship had failed, just that it had run its course. Relationships could work that way.

She opened her brown eyes and flashed me a mischievous smile. "I'd miss you, Amy."

Then again, maybe I was wrong. Maybe we would stay close. You never knew.

• • • •

"What are you doing out here?" Marcus pushed open the screen door. "The sun won't be up for ages."

"Couldn't sleep. Didn't want to wake you." I adjusted myself on the wicker loveseat to make room for him. "Sit with me."

He squeezed in beside me and put his arm around me. "Why can't you sleep?" He kissed my temple. "Got something on your mind?"

"I guess I'm just wondering what the next step will be." I gestured to my laptop, where I had a dozen tabs open to different job listings.

"There's no rush." Marcus ran his fingers through my hair.

"I know. I just want to find the right job. I don't want to leap at the first thing I come across. I want to take my time and end up with something I love. I'd rather do it right the first time."

"You're starting to sound like me," he said.

I laughed. "So you're rubbing off on me."

He chuckled, then leaned his head against mine. "I want you to know, I'm really proud of you, Amy. For finishing this program. For being such a great wife. For everything. You're more than I deserve."

I turned my head to kiss him.

Sometimes I didn't feel like I deserved Marcus, either—but I'd chosen him. Twice. I'd questioned myself, and then I'd come back to him. My life wasn't something that I was just getting swept along in. It was a decision I'd made, and it was a decision I would keep making. This was what I wanted. He was what I wanted.

"I love you," I told him.

And I kissed him again.

• • • •

Final exams finished up a few days before graduation. Corrina would be flying in for the weekend, and Kari and her family would be joining us for dinner at a top-rated seafood restaurant on the bay that Marcus had booked.

I left my last exam feeling exhausted but cleansed. I was coming up on a few days of rest—I just wanted a chance to turn my brain off.

On my way to the car, I checked my phone. I had three new emails, one of which was a reply to an application I'd sent out a few days before.

Dear Amy, it read, *We have received your resume and references and would like to arrange an interview. Please call when your transcripts are available, and we will set up a time for you to meet with our hiring committee.*

The next email was from Professor West.

Dear Amy, I have been impressed with your hard work and profes-
sionalism while in my class, and throughout this research project. If
you are interested in continuing this research and assisting me with
the composition of the book, as well as similar projects in the future,
I would like to extend an offer of employment through the university.
Please call me at your convenience.

I let out a whoop of delight. I should text Marcus. No, I wanted to tell him and the kids in person tonight. I'd call Kari instead.

She answered on the first ring. "Hey, Ames. How was your final?"

"I'm just leaving, and I wanted to tell you that I already received two follow-ups on some applications I sent out." I tried to speak quietly, but I wanted to shout out my good news.

"So you've got choices!" Kari said. "Not that I'm surprised. I knew you'd do great. I'm so happy for you." I heard the crackle of static from her end, and then Ebrahim crying.

"I don't mean to keep you. I just wanted you to be the first to know."

"I'm glad you did! And you should be proud of yourself. The rest of us are, you know." There was another cry from the baby.

"I'll let you go," I said. "I just wanted to share my good news."

"You can tell me more about it this weekend. And maybe by then you'll have made a decision."

"I'll keep you posted," I assured her before hanging up.

I felt wonderful—and why shouldn't I? My life was coming together in a way I couldn't have imagined a few years ago. Then, I'd had to choose between my needs and my family's needs.

Or at least, that was what I'd thought at the time. Maybe I'd been wrong. Maybe taking care of myself was *part* of taking care of my family, part of becoming a better mother and wife. Maybe putting time into my own future would show my children that you could be more than one thing. That you didn't have to settle, or worry about other people's expectations. That you could be whatever and whoever you wanted to be. That if you kept your eyes open to new things and new people, you'd see opportunity coming, and all that could be missed in a blink if they weren't ready.

• • • •

Instead of heading home right away, I dumped my bag in the car and headed down toward the harbor on foot. The day was warm, but the wind coming off the water was cool and brisk, smelling of open air and salt and big horizons.

I stuffed my hands in my pockets and took a deep breath of air. The breeze whipped my hair across my face, and I finally twisted it back into a loose bun to keep it out of my eyes.

It had been years since we left Hawaii. I could remember the beach at Fort DeRussy if I closed my eyes, but the image in my mind was like a picture postcard, a little too perfect to be real. The woman I'd been then was the same way—we looked alike, sure, but we weren't really the same.

The teenager I'd been wouldn't have recognized herself in the young mother standing on the Hawaiian coast. The woman I'd been when the kids were small wouldn't have dreamed she'd grow into me.

I climbed over a low granite wall toward where the water lapped against the concrete shoreline. It was a far cry from white sand beaches you could dig your toes into, but it was nice to stand beside the waves again for a little while.

As a girl, I'd been mesmerized by the push and pull of the ocean, and the way the waves left lines in the sand, traces of the high water marks. All of that motion had seemed like so much work, and I pitied the sea for never being able to stand still.

Today, the certainty of constant movement and the press ever higher made sense to me. It was promising to remember that even the ocean isn't static—there's always the hope of new movement, another foray deeper into the unknown.

Soon enough I'd have to turn back, but not yet. For the moment I could stand there, just breathing, just feeling the sun on my face.

It was good to be loved. To be wanted. To be missed. But some days I didn't want to be rushed. Some days, I wanted to stand in the breeze and look out across the blue sky and the blue water, hunting for the line that separated them, and never being quite sure where it fell.

Chapter Twenty-Four

I left Professor West's office around one o'clock. I'd been typing up notes well past my usual lunch time. There was a cafe only a few blocks away, and I was ready for a coffee and something sweet. Maybe some caffeine and a sugar rush would get me ready to tackle the afternoon.

I pushed the door of the cafe open, still wrapped up in my own thoughts. I walked up to the display of brightly colored confections and debated between a strawberry shortcake bar and a chocolate-dipped brownie.

My skin prickled, and I had the sudden, unnerving sensation that someone was watching me. When I looked around, though, I saw only happy people sipping lattes and chatting, or surfing the Internet on their phones and tablets. I made it through the small crowd around the checkout counter before I stopped short.

Sitting at one of the tables by the window were two men in white hospital coats.

One of them was The Doctor.

He must have gotten that new position, then. His retirement from the military would have gone through before last Christmas. He was deep in conversation with his companion, but he had his eyes glued to me, and when he saw me looking, he smiled.

It had been over a year since I'd seen him.

"Can I get you something?" asked the barista, craning her neck to meet my eye.

"Oh. Yes, sorry. Medium coffee. Um," I glanced over my shoulder to where The Doctor and his friend sat deep in conversation. His presence had left me flustered, and I was no longer hungry.

"Room for cream?"

I nodded mutely.

I stole a quick peek at The Doctor while the barista took my money and retrieved my drink. His work companion no longer sat beside him. It was just The Doctor, leaning back in his chair and watching me. I turned my face away to hide the flush rising in my cheeks and neck. He was giving me a familiar look, one I knew all too well. It was the look he gave me before he kissed me, one full of need and want. He smiled when I met his gaze for a quick moment. What was he thinking? He knew exactly what he was doing to me, and he was clearly enjoying my reactions. Didn't he know that things between us had already run their course?

They had, hadn't they?

Or maybe that was just something I tried to tell myself, because at that moment, all the feelings I'd told myself I no longer felt for him came rushing back. The barista handed me my coffee and I headed for the condiment station. I tried to peek again discreetly as I poured my cream, and this time he nodded in greeting.

I couldn't stop myself from responding with a playful smile. His face lit up, and he gestured for me to come over.

What would I say? Would I hug him? No, I couldn't bear the idea of feeling his body against mine.

Grow up, Amy, I told myself. *Get a grip. You're a big girl.*

I took my coffee and headed over to where he sat. As I approached, he stood to greet me.

"Amy," he said. "It's nice to see you."

His companion stepped out of the bathroom, then headed back to the line for the counter.

"You too." I brushed my hair back from my face. "How have you been?"

"Good. It's been a long time." He paused. "I've missed you."

I wanted to grab him, hold him, kiss him, tell him everything that had happened since the last time I'd seen him. Tell him I missed him so much that it hurt to even acknowledge the memory of him.

"I've missed you too," was all I said.

He took a step closer and reached for my empty hand. With that small physical contact my body recognized his touch. It sent a thrill through me, like touching a live wire. I felt like we were the only two people in the cafe, as if a spotlight had closed in on us and the world outside our bodies was shrouded in darkness.

I looked into his eyes for what felt like a long time. He looked the same as he always had, as if no time had passed, and it made me heartsick.

I took a breath to refocus myself. "How's the new job?"

"Wonderful. Not so new now, of course." He spun his ring on his finger while he talked. An old, familiar habit. "How's . . . everything?"

"I'm working on campus now."

"With that old professor of yours?"

I nodded.

"That's great."

I looked up at his friend who was now at the front of the line. "Actually, I should get back. I'm glad I ran into you, though."

We only had a few more moments alone.

The Doctor sensed this too, because he caught my elbow and lowered his voice. "I look for you in the park every Sunday morning." With each word he spoke, I could feel myself leaning toward him. "I'll be there, rain or shine."

I wasn't ready to let go yet. Instead of answering, I set my coffee on the table and pulled him into a hug.

I'd loved this man. He'd been an important part of my life for so long, someone I'd shared my heart and my body with. He knew more about me than almost anyone, and I wanted to keep that connection alive. Not having him in my life was like missing part of myself. He had given me no reason to stop loving him, and it would be dishonest to tell myself that he didn't still have a place in my heart.

Another part of me knew that our lives no longer fit together, no matter how much I wanted to make room for him. I wasn't the same person I'd been when we met. I wasn't even the same person I'd been the last time I saw him.

But I would never take back what we'd had.

"I'll be waiting for you," he said. He leaned in again and I could feel his breath on my ear. This time our cheeks brushed, and neither of us flinched.

The words hung there between us.

His spoken offer.

And my unspoken choice.

Made in the USA
Middletown, DE
31 July 2021